Critical Acclaim for Eric Koch...

"Eric Koch has been explaining German culture to North America for years."
    - *The Globe and Mail*

"It takes a great deal of imagination, background knowledge, psychological understanding and the talent of a born writer to carry it off. Mr. Koch has done so triumphantly.... Mr. Koch's amazing story, movingly and skilfully told, once again proves that the truth can be stranger than fiction, especially in dark times such as Europe during the thirties and forties."
    - Walter Laqueur

"Eric Koch's brilliant, unique and moving account of two lives has the passion of personal involvement, the clarity of historical observation and the revelation of archetypal drama. It is a remarkable piece of writing."
    - Adrienne Clarkson,
      journalist and former
      Governor-General of Canada

"His imaginative agility, inventiveness and stylish wit have enabled him to create original and highly entertaining works."
    - *Oxford Companion of
      Canadian Literature*

"Conceptually intriguing...Koch's historical novel...is intelligently written and highly informative."
    - *Publishers Weekly*

NEW BEGINNINGS

Library and Archives Canada Cataloguing in Publication

Koch, Eric, 1919-, author
        New beginnings / Eric Koch.

Short stories.
Issued in print and electronic formats.
ISBN 978-1-77161-058-2 (pbk.).--ISBN 978-1-77161-060-5 (pdf).--
ISBN 978-1-77161-059-9 (html)

        I. Title.

PS8521.O23N49 2014   C813'.54   C2014-903498-9
                                              C2014-903499-7

Pubished by Mosaic Press, Oakville, Ontario, Canada, 2014.
Distributed in the United States by Bookmasters (www.bookmasters.com).
Distributed in the U.K. by Gazelle Book Services (www.gazellebookservices.co.uk).

MOSAIC PRESS, Publishers
Copyright © 2014 Eric Koch

Printed and Bound in Canada.
ISBN Paperback 978-1-77161-058-2
          ePub 978-1-77161-060-5
          ePDF 978-1-77161-059-9

Designed by Eric Normann

We acknowledge the financial support of the Government of Canada
through the Canada Book Fund
(CBF) for this project.

Nous reconnaissons l'aide financière
du gouvernement du Canada par
l'entremise du Fonds du livre du
Canada (FLC) pour ce projet.

 Canadian   Patrimoine
Heritage   canadien

 Canada

MOSAIC PRESS
1252 Speers Road, Units 1 & 2
Oakville, Ontario L6L 5N9
phone: (905) 825-2130

info@mosaic-press.com

www.mosaic-press.com

NEW BEGINNINGS

**Tommy Douglas,
Maureen Forrester,
Mackenzie King,
Igor Gouzenko,
Maurice Duplessis,
Camillien Houde,
Vincent Massey
& Andrew Allan**

Eight Stories

Eric Koch

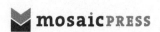

Eric Koch

Other Books by Eric Koch

Now available in eBook format from Mosaic Press

Fiction

*The Golden Years: Encounters with Glenn Gould,
Marshall McLuhan, Lester B. Pearson, René Lévesque
and John G. Diefenbaker*, 2012

The Weimar Triangle, 2010

Premonitions, 2008, 2009

*Arabian Nights 1914:
A Novel about Kaiser Wilhelm II*, 2003

Earrings, 2002

Non-fiction

I Remember the Location Exactly, 2007

Other Books by Eric Koch

Fiction

The French Kiss
McClelland & Stewart, Toronto, 1969

The Leisure Riots
Tundra Books, Montreal, 1973
Die Freizei Revoluzzer*, Heyne Verlag, Munich

The Last Thing You'd Want to Know
Tundra Books, Montreal, 1976
Die Spanne Leben*, Heyne Verlag, Munich
(*Both German versions were reissued together
in 1987 under the title CRUPP.)

Goodnight, Little Spy
Virgo Press, Toronto, and Ram Publishing, London, 1979

Kassandrus
Heyne Verlag, Munich, 1988

Liebe und Mord auf Xananta
Verlag Eichborn, Frankfurt, 1992

Icon in Love: A Novel about Goethe
Mosaic Press, Oakville, 1998

Nobelpreis für Goethe
Fischer Tachenbuch, Frankfurt, 1999

The Man Who Knew Charlie Chaplin
Mosaic Press, Oakville, 2000

L'uomo Chi Splió Hitler, Barbera Editoré, Siena, 2006

Non-fiction

Deemed Suspect
Methuen, Toronto, 1980

Inside Seven Days
Prentice-Hall, Toronto, 1986

Hilmar and Odette
McClelland & Stewart, Toronto, 1996
Chongqing Publishing House, 1998

The Brothers Hambourg
Robin Brass, Toronto, 1997

Die Braut im Zwielicht: Erinnerungen
Weidle Verlag, Bonn, 2009

Table of Contents

Preface

There is no shortage of non-fictional literature about the eight characters who are the subjects of these stories. But if you are in search of "truth" and are in the mood for entertainment you may prefer to read these stories. They are no less "true" and will save you time.

I wrote them to convey the essence of their personalities. I wanted to convey, as vividly as I could, the role they played at a time when the seeds were sown of the Canada we know.

The thread connecting them is the ingenious and enterprising narrator who is pure invention, just like the narrator of the five stories in The Golden Years which appeared a year ago. The other subsidiary characters are also invented, except Henning Andersen in the Gouzenko story. He is modeled on Henning Sorensen, the head of the Dutch Section of the CBC's International Service (now call RCI) when I was head of the German Section. His testimony is contained in the Report of the Kellock-Taschereau Commission.

Eric Koch

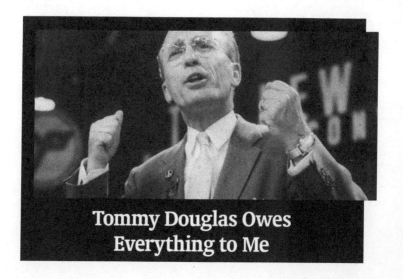

**Tommy Douglas Owes
Everything to Me**

In early September 1943 I heard from several philosophical fellow-scholars that the University of Toronto was sending a train load of students to Saskatchewan to help with the harvest. Since many, if not most, able-bodied men were overseas there was a severe shortage of labour. I had been diagnosed with a murmur of the heart and was not able to join up. No news could have been more welcome and I heroically signed on.

Most of the students who had also volunteered were urban types like me and had acquired whatever knowledge they had of western farming from the movies. I had been in Europe several times, and often in New York, but had never been further west than Oakville. So it was about time I went. Moreover, if I was lucky—and I often was—I hoped that Joe McTaggert, the farmer in Lucky Pond—aptly named, I assumed—near Weyburn in whose barn I was to be billeted, knew something about the Saskatchewan CCF, which was said to be in the forefront of advanced thinking about postwar Canada. Even here in stuffy old Ontario the CCF had made a big breakthrough in 1942 when it became the official opposition. The unknown school teacher Joe Noseworthy had decisively defeated the former Tory prime minister Arthur Meighen in York South.

I found the two days and two nights on the transcontinental train by no means too long. I was in boisterous company, largely thanks to the engineering students who brought with them a treasure of bawdy songs:

Hitler, he only has one ball,
Goering, he has two but very small,
Himmler has something simmler,
But poor old Goebbels has no balls at all.

I loved that song, even the tenth time we sang it while passing through the forests and along the lakes of Northern Ontario until we came to the Prairies, when we became entirely dependent on the fortunately inexhaustible repertoire of the engineers.

In Weyburn about a dozen farmers were waiting for us with their trucks. It was late afternoon. We were divided up. I was one of the three philosophers assigned to McTaggert, a worn-out middle-aged man with a sad, lined face who looked us over without much enthusiasm and then said, no doubt to stifle any false expectations, "You won't find many books here."

"That is not why we came, Mr. McTaggert," I tried to reassure him on the way to his truck. "We have more than enough books at home. We came to help."

"Well, we'll see about that," he mumbled. "I'm Joe. Nobody's called me Mr. McTaggert for twenty years. And my wife is Anne."

The uncomfortable truck ride took at least two hours while it was slowly getting dark. We were in the back, no one sat in the good front next to Joe. The truck had no springs. There was acute disagreement among us whether the half-harvested fields we passed grew wheat, oats, barley or flax. We left the question open. There was a strong chilly wind. We passed a number of dilapidated, abandoned buildings and a few barely legible signs. It was not clear whether they were names of farms or habitations of some sort—Bison, Riel, Blackfoot.

At last we arrived. Joe took us directly to the barn, pointed to the outhouse at the back and told us to wash up at the well and then come to the house for dinner. In the airless, hay-filled barn three bunks awaited us, covered with blankets and pillows. In our studies we had specialized in stoicism. Throughout our stay in Lucky Pond we did not complain about anything, not even among ourselves.

Mrs. Anne McTaggert was everything her husband was not. She was cheerful, lively, engaging and interested in the outside world and she took a motherly interest in her guests. There was also a silent but ravishing girl, eighteen years old, an evacuee from Canterbury by the name of Penny. Both had prepared a generous and tasty dinner that they served, unfortunately, not sitting down with us men—they ate after we left. We each fervently hoped that sooner or later we would have the opportunity to break Penny's silence. The ample ham and potato dinner, the various vegetables and salads, and especially the climactic apple pie, all this stood in dramatic contrast to the sparseness of the furniture in the poverty-stricken house. We sat on orange crates and spare tires. Evidently, the McTaggerts had not yet recovered from the drought and the Depression and could not yet afford to buy chairs. It was quite possible that they received a subsidy to feed us.

The next morning at five thirty our amiable hostess came to the barn to rouse us. She had already done a number of chores. We barely managed to comply. However, our spirits revived when we were served an amazing breakfast—juice, bacon, eggs, potatoes, fresh coffee. The lovely Penny remained silent.

After breakfast Joe drove us out into the field and told us what to do—to stoop down and, with the help of rakes, gather the wheat into stooks so that later, after the sun was out and the dew had been burned off, they could be gathered by the rented threshing machine.

The first two hours were tolerable, but by the time the sun was out my back hurt so much that I could hardly bend it any more. My friends did no better. We did not complain—we just groaned. When Joe came to pick us up at four and looked at the meagre results of our efforts, he just grumbled something unintelligible, which no doubt meant that he hoped we were better at book-learning. We could hardly sit up during our second dinner. I asked Penny whether she would give us a massage, which we desperately needed for our sore backs, but she merely smiled sweetly and shook her gorgeous head. Efforts to unfreeze her would have to wait for another day. Anne said, no doubt correctly, the first day was always the most difficult for people who weren't used to farm work.

The next morning we were surprised to note that we could rise from our bunks and even stand up and walk upright to the outhouse. At breakfast Penny rewarded us for this achievement by speaking to us for the first time, going as far as to say, "Would you like another cup of coffee?"

When Joe drove us out she even waved to us.

I called out to her while Joe switched on the ignition, *Morituri te salutant*! She laughed and said—yes, she actually spoke again—she had taken Latin at school in Canterbury.

Things were looking up!

The second day was bad but a little better than the first.

As for Penny, it was impossible to know what actually had brought about the change in her—it did not really matter. She was positively voluble at dinner.

"Are you interested in politics?" I tested her.

"As a matter of fact I am," she replied eagerly.. "My father is a Labour MP."

All of us students sat up. We asked her to tell us more. She had a brother fighting in Italy under General Alexander. Her father had fought at the Somme in the Great War and was on several military committees in the House of Commons. She grew up in a family where politics was discussed every day at dinner.

"Penny has been telling me about her family," Anne told us. "We are so happy she came to us."

For once Joe spoke too.

"I agree," he said. "Very fine family. Good socialists, like us."

"That's right," Anne went on. "Just for Penny I have invited our member in the Legislature for dinner tomorrow. He was chosen the leader of the CCF at the convention earlier this year. I went to school with his wife, Irma. She's coming, too. You'll enjoy meeting both of them."

I knew I would be lucky in Lucky Pond.

"Oh what a good idea," I exclaimed. "I was hoping to learn something about Saskatchewan politics while I'm here. What's his name?"

"Tommy Douglas. He was our preacher at the Calvary Baptist Church in Weyburn. Everybody says he was the best preacher in the West. And certainly the funniest. Born in Glasgow, maybe that's why. Irma and I met him at Brandon College. He was our member in Ottawa for a number of years, but he came back home to lead the

CCF here. A most determined politician. Well, you'll see for yourselves."

The prospect of meeting this man, and asking him what kind of revolution he expected after the war, made my third day of back-breaking labour endurable. It suddenly became remotely conceivable that eventually we might actually make a tangible contribution to saving Joe's harvest.

"What kind of revolution?"

The amusing little Scottish preacher-politician chuckled as he buttered the bread that Anne had baked for the occasion. In his and Irma's honour Anne and Penny sat at the table with us while a neighbour's wife and her rather plain daughter served. I had popped my question directly after we had finished the tomato soup. "Red? Blue? Green? White? Do you think Irma and I will be able to go to a store in downtown Weyburn and pick the revolution of our choice? Which colour would you pick, Irma?"

"I'd like mine beige." Mrs. Douglas's eyes were sparkling behind her glasses. "Definitely beige."

Her husband turned to me.

"What makes you so sure we'll have a revolution?"

"In Toronto we can't go the movies on Sundays," I responded. "The young will rise against the old. In Montreal the French will rise against the English because they forced them to go to a war 'for the English king'. And they will rise against the church. I want to know what will happen here."

Tommy rubbed his prominent chin.

"What do you think will happen in England, Penny?" he asked.

"We'll abolish the capitalist system," she said without a moment's hesitation. "I mean, it really already finished itself off when it caused the Depression. We'll give it the final kick in the teeth."

"Hear, hear," said Joe.

"Well, I am a hundred percent with you," Tommy Douglas said. "But I wish I knew how to do it. Do you, Penny?"

"Of course," she said. "I would take one step at a time. I would appeal to everybody's better instincts. Persuade people to cooperate instead of putting all the emphasis on competition."

Tommy beamed.

"I couldn't have said it better myself," he said. "I was afraid you were going to say 'gather all the capitalists at Piccadilly Circus and hang them'."

Everybody laughed.

Tommy turned to me.

"You seem to be a bright young man with a lively imagination. Are you prepared to save my political life?"

"The answer is yes, of course," I said. "If I can. What do you have in mind?"

"I want you to go to the visitors' gallery in the Legislature in Regina next Monday and accuse me of being a communist. None of the dummies in the Liberal or Tory parties ever give me a proper chance to make it clear that socialists are not communists."

"I'll do my best," I said. "If Joe will let me go."

Joe nodded. "Sure. I'll arrange it."

"But how would my performance save your political life?" I asked.

"Because there's one man at the top of my very own party who wants to cut my throat. He thinks I'm a communist. We'll never get anywhere unless I speak up clearly in the Legislature—and demonstrate to the whole world—that I'm in Penny's camp. I'm in favour of evolution, not revolution."

I turned to Joe.

"Would you allow Penny to come with me if she wants to?"

"Sure," Joe said. "Why not?" He turned to Penny. "Do you want to?"

Penny clapped her hands.

"Of course," she exclaimed. "What an adventure!"

            🐛   🐛   🐛

Penny and I were the only visitors in the visitors' gallery.

Way below, Tommy was in full swing. He was speaking about public health.

"Mr. Speaker, does any member of this Legislative Assembly not know that people with money can secure the medical services and hospital care they need while people without money cannot?"

"Stick to the subject," a member on the front bench demanded. "We're talking abut Bill 112."

"I'm sorry, Mr. Speaker, this is very much to the point. There's no point enlarging the hospital in Moose Jaw unless we face the fact that we have all the facilities, right in the honourable member's riding, and yet only the rich can afford them and there are very few of them."

This was my cue.

"Eh, you down there!" I shouted at the top of my voice. "Why don't you go home to Moscow where you belong?"

"Well done!" Penny whispered to me.

"What was that?" Tommy cocked his ear. "Do I hear the voice of the people?"

"You certainly do," I went on shouting. "If people like you had their way you would have the state seize every farmer's land, close down all the banks, seize everybody's savings and shut down every parliament! You'd crush democracy and establish a dictatorship of the proletariat run by little creeps like you."

Tommy was silent. No one had a better sense of theatre. He allowed an entire minute for the full significance of my words to sink in.

Slowly, the Liberal premier John William Patterson rose. His reputation of being singularly unimpressive seemed wholly justified.

"The people have spoken," he said with a faint smile. "I note that for once the Leader of the Opposition is tongue tied."

"Come on, Douglas," a front bencher demanded. "Say something."

"It is not often," Tommy began, speaking slowly at first, "that this House has the benefit of words of profound wisdom uttered by a no doubt distinguished visitor who, without a word of reprimand from the Speaker, is permitted to break all the rules of civilized debate. These very rules do not allow me to suggest that the Speaker may be biased on the side of those who accuse 'little creeps' like me of being an 'enemy of freedom'. Therefore I suggest we will for once allow Mr. Speaker to get away with it."

"Thank you," the Speaker smiled. "No doubt if you were in my shoes you would have the 'distinguished visitor'"—all eyes went up to me—"forcibly seized and arrested."

"No, Mr. Speaker," Tommy said. "I would do no such thing. I would have him drawn and quartered. Now let me reply to him. No, sir. You mention Moscow. As I understand it, Moscow is the home of communists. You seem to think that I would feel at home with communists in Moscow. Is that right?"

This time the Speaker intervened.

"The honourable member knows very well that he cannot conduct a dialogue with a visitor in the visitors gallery. Would he please cease and desist."

"Yes, Mr. Speaker. I will abide by the rules of the House and I am grateful to you that you administer them so faithfully. We socialists have nothing in common with communists—except one thing. We also believe that those who have money and privilege should share their wealth with those who do not. But we think that these goals can be achieved through evolution, not revolution, by persuasion, not force, by cooperation not competition, without confiscating anybody's private property, in the conviction that God gave us all the power of reason, the common sense, the inborn feeling for justice, to make this possible. No force is needed because if things are explained properly it will be obvious to everybody. Only those will oppose us who prefer their own welfare to that of the rest of us, and we all know what the gospels have to say about greed and selfishness. Communists don't believe in persuasion. We do because we believe free people will choose the right course simply by reason of being free. I am grateful to you, Mr. Speaker, for having given me the opportunity to state my case for once without the usual interruptions."

There was a roar of thunderous applause from Tommy's followers.

៛   ៛   ៛

In the truck on back to Joe's farm Penny gave every sign of thoroughly enjoying my passionate kisses.

And in the following spring, on June 15, 1944, Tommy Douglas led his party to victory. The CCF got 53 percent of the vote and 47 of the 53 seats in the Saskatchewan Legislature. He immediately offered the man who was going to cut his throat a seat in the Cabinet.

And he sent me a note saying that he owed his victory entirely to me.

The Emergence
of Maureen Forrester

In the early spring of 1953 I tore myself away from my new girlfriend, Holly, for an hour and visited André Lavigne in his spacious but invitingly sleazy office on Clark Street in Montreal. I wanted to know how he was doing.

Montreal was an "Open City," which means that it had a Red Light District. This was the part of town in which André had important commercial interests.

I had met him just after the war. He was the uncle of one of the few French Canadian students at the University of Toronto. My friend was amused, and in no way embarrassed, by his uncle's dubious sources of income. I must confess that for us Anglo-Saxons, even for a young and enlightened Anglo-Saxon like me, that seemed a little strange.

On this visit, once again, I observed how much like a small-town dentist André looked, in such dramatic contrast to the sleazy grandeur of his office and the lofty scope of his licit and illicit enterprises.

"Things are changing fast around here," he told me after we had settled down. "Hardly anybody wants to become a priest any more and there is a serious shortage of nuns."

We spent a few minutes discussing the implications of this and related phenomena.

"How is Pauline doing?" I asked at last.

Pauline Désy was André's elegant friend and business partner, the co-owner of their houses on de Bullion Street.

"Pauline is at her best in times of adversity," he smiled, stroking his little mustache. "The demand is still pretty impressive but since City Hall has suddenly discovered Virtue, the poor girl and her labour force have had to go underground. And it didn't help, of course, that *Le Devoir* has recently been so unkind to the police, suddenly accusing them of corruption, of all things—as though this was going to make any difference. I hate hypocrisy more than anything else. But don't worry. Pauline will manage."

André paused.

"Do you mind if we talk about something else?" he asked. "I am very glad you came to see me today because there is something you can do for me. You can help me with a different kind of business project. Something requiring unusual tact and diplomacy."

"You're a master at both, André," I laughed. "How can I do better?"

"I don't need your flattery, young man. I am serious. No, this is something I cannot do. You may not know that I am very fond of music, especially Italian opera."

"Oh? No, I didn't know that." Holly, too, is musical and constantly teases me because I can't carry a tune.

"About two weeks ago somebody told me about a young girl with a great voice who was born a few blocks east of here, on the rue Fabre. Just drive east on the boulevard St. Joseph until you come to the Église St. Stanislas, and you'll see the row house in which she was brought up—in a three-room apartment. Very poor. Her mother is Irish, her father Scottish. Protestant. She was the youngest of four. Dropped out of high school at thirteen. Took all kinds of jobs, from selling ice cream to being a Bell Telephone operator. She's now twenty-three. Even today she still hands over to her family most of the little money she makes, singing in church choirs, at weddings and giving solo recitals. A few thousand dollars would make all the difference. She could stop singing for money and spend all her time studying. Her teachers say that if she carries on this way she will ruin her voice and never get anywhere."

"Have you heard her sing?"

"I have. I most certainly have. She is incredible. A contralto, warm and clear and very expressive. I know enough to be able to tell that her teachers are right and that she has the voice and the talent to become an international star. But she is proud and strong-willed and will not accept any help she considers charity."

"You amaze me, André," I said. "I would never have expected you to take on this sort of project. I am really impressed."

"That goes to show that you've got to be very careful about making assumptions. In fact, that is exactly the point."

"The point of what?"

"The point of my problem. I am too well known. Everybody makes assumptions. So probably does she. I have not the slightest doubt that the girl has heard of me and my association with Pauline. Everybody has. She would never accept help from me even if it's made clear to her that it's not charity I have in mind, but a business investment in her future. There's no point asking her."

"I see the problem," I observed. "You are right. This requires tact and diplomacy. And ingenuity. What's her name?"

"Maureen Forrester."

"Give me a day to think about it, André."
"But remember, one false move and you'll ruin everything."
"Don't worry."

ॐ   ॐ   ॐ

Discussing the matter with Holly was far from a false move. One of the men I had often heard her rave about, John Newmark, happened to be Maureen Forrester's accompanist. Small world. Life is full of little coincidences.

Holly was the most bohemian girlfriend I ever had, and one of the most alluring. She was gorgeous, looked like a model, dressed like a model and, in fact, occasionally was a model. Most models are boring and conventional, but Holly was the opposite. She was maddeningly unpredictable and always late. Her most common term of abuse was "bourgeois." Anybody or anything bourgeois was despicable beyond belief. She was a delightful flirt and great fun to be with (when she finally turned up for a date). For many weeks she always averted her head when I tried to kiss her, even though she said she loved going out with me. Whenever that happened I just shrugged and thought that for the moment the pleasure of her company on dates was enough.

Holly adored the glamorous and handsome John Newmark, universally known in the world of music, I was told, as one of the greatest and most sensitive accompanists in the world today. She first met him when she lined up to see him after a concert, congratulated him on his playing and said if ever he needed a page turner on the stage, she would love to do it and gave him her phone number. He called her the next morning and booked her for the following Tuesday afternoon for a recital by George London at the Ladies' Morning Musical Concert Series at the Ritz Carlton Hotel.

Newmark was a refugee from Germany and had already been an accomplished pianist before the Nazis came to power. He often talked about his exciting life in the Berlin of Marlene Dietrich.

After her successful début as a page turner, Holly often met prominent music lovers in Newmark's elegant apartment at 1454 Crescent Street, just north of St. Catherine Street and exactly opposite the spot where Roncarelli's restaurant had been.

When I told Holly about André's problem at dinner, she suggested two things. First, I should talk to John and then call Eric McLean, the music critic of the *Montreal Star* and sound him out.

"Just ask John directly whether he thinks André was right when he said that one can't discuss his proposition with the girl. John knows her well. I'll introduce you if you like. I'll phone him right now."

After three minutes she was back.

"He'll give us tea tomorrow afternoon at four thirty. At five what's-her-name is coming to rehearse with him. When you meet her you can play it by ear."

I phoned Eric McLean from home. I remembered meeting him at a party not long ago. I mentioned Maureen without saying a word about André. As soon as I began telling him what I knew about her, he stopped me. It so happened he had just written a piece about the girl, which would appear in tomorrow's paper.

I was, of course, delighted to hear it—that could only help whatever my next move would be.

The next day Holly and I went to tea at John Newmark's in his impeccably kept apartment. The pianist, wearing a light blue ascot and a maroon velvet jacket, welcomed me with just the right combination of bonhomie and caution. The tea and delectable petits fours were ready.

"Oh John," Holly exclaimed as she helped herself. "You're so *bourgeois*!"

"Too bad," he laughed. "That's the way God made me."

He had a slight German accent, less noticeable, Holly told me later, when he spoke French than when he spoke English.

Over the grand piano there was a painting of a forest scene he had just bought from a friend of his, Max Stern, the owner of the Dominion Gallery on Sherbrooke Street. The painter was Emily Carr. Dr. Stern had recently discovered her in British Columbia.

"So what is all this about?" John turned to me.

I told him all, including, of course, André's involvement in his dubious enterprises.

"Ouch," he cried, as though he had just stubbed his toe. "She'll never accept money from him. She needs an angel, but not from a character like that."

"Why not?" Holly asked. "Is she such a prude? Doesn't she know money is money?"

"Don't be so cynical, young lady," John rebuked her. "Money is *not* money."

"I accept money from anybody," Holly shot back. "For anything."

"Isn't there a way around it?" I asked. "Perhaps one could establish a trust fund or something like that. All her friends could contribute. She would never find out which ones."

"She would, she would," John said. "In the end this man won't be able to resist boasting about her. Maureen is unique. I have worked with dozens of excellent young singers, in Europe and here. Only one of them had similar natural gifts and instinctive understanding. And that is Kathleen Ferrier. But Maureen is her equal. A glorious voice. And what a marvellous temperament and determination! And—how shall I put it? What *goodness*. Generosity. Humanity. Good humour. Gutsiness. Call it what you want. For her, the music and the meaning of the words she sings always come first, in whatever language."

John poured another cup of tea. "And what stage presence! And no stage fright, ever. And considerable acting talent as well—she'll be great in opera. Especially comic roles. No nervousness at all. And no prima donna tantrums. A real trooper. Amazing! The public all over the world will love her. The greatest conductors will fight over her. She'll be booked two, three years in advance."

He paused for a moment.

"It's a miracle how a talent like that can emerge from such an unlikely background. It really gives one hope. This sort of thing can happen anywhere, any time. No one can tell in advance. For her, this is the right time, and Canada the right place, just when things are beginning to sprout. Mind you, some of her gifts she seems to have inherited from her mother."

He held up a finger. "But without training, and years of hard work and sacrifice, all this will evaporate. And she needs a lot of money and support. Oh my God, things can go wrong so easily. Her family makes tremendous demands on her. I have no idea how she is coping with that. I understand her father has just had a stroke. That's certainly something to worry about. And then, of course, she can fall in love with the wrong man."

"Come on, John," Holly cried. "One thing at a time. She can also catch the bubonic plague."

The doorbell rang.

Maureen Forrester came in, a little out of breath. John helped her with her coat. She was a tall girl, wholesome, agreeable without being beautiful, a little on the plump side. She wore a pleasant blue dress.

John made the introductions. Holly he described as his most talented page turner, and me as the page turner's faithful escort who may also have a great career as a page turner himself if he works hard.

"Nothing doing," I declared. "I can't read a note."

"You don't need to," Holly said. "John always gives a little nod."

"Have a little something to eat." John offered Maureen the plate of petits fours. "You need strength for the Schubert. My friends will leave in a minute. Unless they first want to ask you a question."

"Don't go," she said, without listening to John. "You must hear my story. Did you see Eric McLean's piece in the *Star* today?"

No, we had not.

"It's quite a long piece, all about me, and he gave me hell." She pulled it out of her handbag and handed it to us. "He said I was doing all the wrong things, singing all over the place and spreading myself too thin. That at my age I should be studying and expanding my repertoire. Such a taxing schedule could threaten a beginner's voice and health. He says I should stop singing in public immediately."

She put the paper away and looked at John.

"Did you tell him to write that?" she asked.

"No, I most certainly did not," he said. "On the contrary, I think Eric is asking for a lot."

"He sure is. Anyway, this morning I got a call from Mr. McConnell's secretary. He's the publisher of the *Star*, you know. I should go and see him right away. So I did. He's about eighty. He said he has been interested in me for some time. Somebody had told him that I was supporting my family with my singing. When he read Eric McLean's piece in today's paper he decided to have a little talk with me. He said it was probably unrealistic to expect me to stop singing in public, as his music critic demanded, but did he not have a good point? How did I manage financially?"

Holly poked me sharply in the ribs.

"And what did you say to the old man?" John asked.

"I said yes, I would find it painful to stop singing right now, as his Mr. McLean demanded, just as I am beginning to get steady engagements and build a reputation. My real problem is that my performances are costing me more than I am earning. Sometimes my fee is only twenty-five dollars. By the time I pay for my transportation and get my hair done and buy a pair of nylons, there is nothing left."

"I hope," John interrupted, "you also mentioned that your accompanist had to have enough money to buy petits fours. Although of course he could bake them himself."

"John, please be serious. I said my expenses for sheet music are as much as four hundred dollars a year, and of course there is still the price of my singing lessons twice a week. I am constantly in the red. There are times I hate to answer the door in case it is the bank manager announcing another overdraft. And do you know what Mr. McConnell said? He asked me whether I would allow him to cover all my deficits, on condition that I didn't tell anybody. He didn't want every mother with a talented child on his doorstep."

"We won't tell a soul," Holly said. "Will we?"

"No," I promised. "We won't."

"After I told him that I was flabbergasted by his offer," Maureen continued, "he disappeared into his own private washroom and came back wearing a ratty old brown tweed jacket with leather patches on the elbows and sleeves that were too short for him."

"You know, I, too, was poor once," he announced. "This was my first jacket."

☙   ☙   ☙

This story has a happy ending. Maureen accepted the offer. John and Holly were delighted, and so was André.

"After what *Le Devoir* did to me," he exclaimed when I told him about it, "all I can say is that I hope the *Star* behaves better. "I don't trust anybody in the press."

The Inner Life of Mackenzie King

I owe it to an odd encounter that I became one of the few Canadians who found out about William Lyon Mackenzie King's spiritualism before everybody else. That odd encounter occurred in 1947, a year before he retired. He died three years later, at seventy-two. That is when it was revealed that he had been talking to the dead regularly since 1932.

Mackenzie King had been prime minister, off and on, for twenty-two years. Now, in retrospect, many thought that his belief in spiritualism was the only thing that made this boring, conventional, uncharismatic man unusual. Suddenly he became very, very interesting—and very, very weird.

The odd encounter occurred when I was living in Ottawa, having managed to get a job as private secretary to C.D. Howe, the minister of reconstruction in charge of steering the delicate transition between the war and the postwar economy. There were to be "jobs for all"—that was his promise. In conjunction with the Bank of Canada, he was to keep inflation in check.

I was on contract, not on staff, which suited me fine. The position enabled me to pick up profitable investment tips. There was, of course, something inherently delightful in being able to pass confidential information to my friends.

Almost every day I had lunch in the cafeteria of the Château Laurier rather than at Murray's or some of the more modest little places around the government buildings. The cafeteria was the favourite lunch place of several mandarins all very much aware that their incomes were a fraction of those paid for equivalent positions in private enterprise. Visiting businessmen holding comparable positions in the private sector preferred to have lunch in the main dining room with suitably obsequious waiters.

I had heard that occasionally Prime Minister Mackenzie King himself turned up in the cafeteria but I never saw him there. My boss, cost-conscious C.D. Howe, was among those who went there frequently, and so did other Cabinet ministers. They all knew the friendly food dispensers at the counter by their first names, Marie-Thérèse and Albert. Occasionally I shared a table with Dr. Milo Schmolka, a pleasant Czech refugee now employed in the Ministry of Health. He told me once how amazed he was after he arrived in Ottawa to discover that Cabinet ministers would appear at this place without any security protection at all, and had done so right through the war, and lined up, tray in hand, with the common people. He said this would have been unheard of in his country, or, for that matter, anywhere in Europe. That is why he wanted to stay in Canada. I enjoyed teasing him and replied that this should not be the only reason why Canada was a good country to come to. Surely Prime Minister Mackenzie King was another.

"Oh, that pudgy little man?" he smiled. "Why do you say that? I have nothing against him. Nobody seems to have anything good to say about him, but everybody votes for him. His most significant characteristic seems to be that he is so prudent that he takes six pairs of shoelaces with him when he travels. In all other respects, isn't he singularly uninteresting?"

"Exactly," I replied. "That is the point. Haven't we had enough of interesting leaders? Fortunately there are only few left."

One week after that conversation I had the odd encounter I mentioned. I was standing in line cheerfully discussing the morning's stock prices with the man ahead of me, an accountant in the defence department, while others recited hockey scores.

A plump, middle-aged lady behind us overheard me.

"You like the stock market?" she whispered to me after Albert had filled my plate with shepherd's pie and Marie-Thérèse had added rice pudding, and handed the accountant a plate with spaghetti covered with tomato sauce.

"Come and sit with me. Maybe you can give me a few tips."

"I'll do what I can," I said, as we sat down at a table behind a potted fern. She reminded me vaguely of a woman I had recently met at a pub on Slater Street who wanted me to invest in an emerald mine in West Africa. This lady said her name was Joan Campbell, Mrs. Joan Campbell, and she had been working for Mr. Mackenzie King for fifteen years.

"Oh really?" I said. "I am very pleased to meet you."

"You have a nice face, young man," she went on. "I think we can probably help one another. Have you any relations with the press?"

"Yes," I replied more or less truthfully. "I know a few people. Why do you ask"

"Because if you give me a few useful tips I have a great story for you. You can sell it you anybody you like. I can't do this myself. You'll understand in a minute why."

Naturally, my curiosity was aroused.

She told me that last week Mr. King asked the personnel people to transfer her to another department. It was true she couldn't get on with the new secretary who had recently come in, very much her junior. For some obscure reason, the PM preferred the new person.

"Is that typical of him?" I asked.

"No, not at all," Joan Campbell said. "He has always been the kindest, most considerate boss. This is most untypical. I'll probably never find out why he did it. He's very secretive, you know. I may not look it but I am very, very angry. I want to make him suffer. And that's where you come in."

"What do you want me to do?"

"I am going to give you some information. As I told you, you may sell it to any of your contacts in the press. You'll make a lot of money."

"Information?" I frowned. "What information?"

"For the last fifteen years the prime minister has been talking to the dead. To his mother, father, brother and sister, and to his great friend Bert Harper, who drowned in the Ottawa River many years ago while trying to save the life of a woman. And to Sir Wilfrid Laurier, and President Roosevelt. But mainly to his mother."

I could not believe my ears.

"Yes," she continued. "He is a believer in spiritualism. And a practitioner. He has spoken to me about it quite freely, many times, over many years. Only a few others know about it. He always emphasizes that he never allows these experiences to influence his political decisions. They are an entirely private matter."

"I can't believe it," I exclaimed. "Nor will anybody else."

I was by no means sure I should have anything to do with this revelation. The idea that while our troops were risking their lives on the battlefield while their leader was communing with the Beyond...

"Oh yes, a lot of people will believe it," Mrs. Campbell insisted. "This is by no mans as odd as you think. Everybody has an old aunt who attends séances. Queen Victoria did."

I was silent for a few moments, deep in thought.

"How do you imagine I proceed?" I asked at last. "I have nothing in writing. No proof."

"I'll give you the name of one of the people in whom he confides."

She opened her handbag and fished out a card.

"Margaret Lewis will tell them all they need to know. She's a one of the mediums he used to engage and has nothing to lose. Mediums have become unpopular and she now makes her living working in a shoe store. Too many of them are no longer trusted. In the last few years Mr. King, too, is one of the spiritualists who has done without mediums. He now believes in direct communications, without any intermediaries. Whatever you do, you must not use my name. It would ruin my career. Now, what tip can you give me in return?"

I had by no means decided to go ahead with her proposition. I was not sure it was a patriotic thing to do. Also, at first glance it seemed too big and explosive for me to handle. But I saw no reason not to give her a quid pro quo for the stick of dynamite she had just placed in my hands.

"Buy plutonium," I said. "But don't tell anybody else about it. Now that Chalk River has broken the American atomic monopoly every ounce of plutonium will be worth a fortune. Your broker will know how to go about it. And buy copper."

"Thanks. I've got to go." She fished out another card from her purse. "This is my home number. And how do I get hold of you?"

I told her. She got up and left.

I ordered another cup of coffee, lit a cigarette, and tried to think what to do next. Ah yes, why not have a drink with my old college friend Herbert Sloan. He was a biologist who worked in the National Research Council—very left wing, and well informed politically. Mackenzie King was his bête noir.

We met that evening after dinner at a pub near his digs at the corner of Bank Street and Third Avenue. He was a tall man with a freckled face and a quick smile, who wore his usual well-worn brown jacket with leather patches on his elbows.

I gave him the facts and asked whether it was a responsible thing to do to shake the nation's confidence in its leader, just to make a few dollars. Why not leave it to others, I asked, or wait until the man retires or dies?

Herbert did not seem at all surprised by what I had just told him.

"I wouldn't hesitate for a minute," he said. "Whatever harm his occult hocus-pocus has done has been done. Go right ahead. It will show everybody what a third-rate character he is."

"I don't really understand it at all," I observed. "King appears to be so rational, the very opposite of naive and gullible. Obviously, Canada has done very well under a prime minister who talks to the dead—but who is also a shrewd, successful politician, very much in control, a man apparently endowed with a lot of common sense. How is common sense compatible with ... what you call occult hocus-pocus?"

"My guess is it is perfectly compatible. He has put his hocus-pocus on one side and everything else on the other. Just as your lady says. I doubt very much that Voices from the Beyond dictated to him every lousy move he has made since he entered politics. He decided all by himself to side with the rich and not with the poor, while acquiring an invaluable and of course entirely undeserved reputation of being a fair-minded conciliator. No wonder he is said to be a wealthy man. He has always known on which side his bread is buttered. And he wants to appear as a man of faith to make us believe that faith is more important than anything else."

"Does he say that?"

"Probably not. He avoids saying anything as definite as that. Just as he avoids involving a lot of people in his decision making. Only capitalists and managers need information, and he happily provides them with it. Everybody else can live on faith. Welfare depends on the philanthropy of men like his friend the late John D. Rockefeller. His beloved grandfather, the William Lyon Mackenzie, must have been turning in his grave all these years. Now there was a rebellious populist for you. Unlike his grandson. Always remember that King entered politics from a position quite high up in the civil service, and that once he was an insider he built his own machine in the civil service and made it part of he government. He is a bureaucrat, wielding power primarily because he can give people jobs and a politician only in times of election. But I admit he is a good judge of character, and knows how to pick capable, loyal people to run his government. He can do this very well all on his own, without any help from the Beyond. Go ahead and publish. The Opposition will love you for it. Maybe you can even help us get rid of him. It's about time. The truth will set us free."

So much for Sloan. I must admit he was very persuasive. I could easily phone Pierre Berton—I knew him slightly—and ask him how much he would pay me for this story. There was no point in asking my boss what to do. C.D. Howe would throw me out of his office at the very hint of disloyalty. Nor would he believe a word of the story. Should I go to the governor general and suggest to him that a man who indulges in occult practices was constitutionally unfit to be prime minister of Canada?

No, before doing any such foolish thing I had to understand—really understand—how a seemingly rational person could behave like that. I had no experience at all in that world. What about phoning the ex-medium, the shoe saleslady Margaret Lewis whose business card was in my wallet? No, most likely she did not get all my points and had her own axes to grind.

I had to talk to an independent, educated person who liked Mackenzie King, who knew about his disposition, did not disapprove of it and could explain it. I did some discreet phoning and at last was given the name of Miss Catherine Surrey, a North Toronto high school principal who was a close friend of a distant cousin. She was in touch with King mainly by letter but occasionally they met.

I happened to know several people who had gone to her school. She immediately agreed to see me in her office.

I took a bus to Toronto.

Catherine Surrey was a friendly, formidable no-nonsense woman with a double chin, no doubt an excellent administrator and teacher, although the less robust of her students must have been in awe of her. Her specialty, she told me, was the Victorian novel, a subject, alas, of limited interest to her students. There was something vaguely Dickensian about her.

I gave her the reasons why I came to see her.

"You are talking to the right person," she smiled. "I have a lot to say about Mackenzie King. First of all, I am appalled by that secretary of his you mentioned. I would want to make her suffer. That's quite awful behaviour, I must say. But let's not waste time on her. Her calculation is all wrong. The nation will not be at all shocked if this matter is presented to it in the right way when the time comes. By you or by anybody else. The people should be told that Canada has a prime minister who has always tried to lead a Christian life and who has done his best to put his Christian beliefs into practice. His interest in spiritualism is an aspect of his Christian beliefs."

I was amazed.

"What an extraordinary way to put it," I observed.

"Not at all. That's where that secretary, and—if I may say so—you got it wrong. You have to see these things in the proper context. Like everything else, religion is subject to fashion. Mr. King was born in 1874, in Victorian Canada. The family was deeply religious—Presbyterian, you know. And very happy. He had an unusually happy childhood. When he went to the University of Toronto, into the Department of Political Economy—class of 1895—and later when he did graduate work at Chicago and Harvard, he was firmly committed to ideas of social, progressive Christianity, and very much involved in questions of welfare, poverty and housing. He was determined to devote his life to improving the lives of others, as a minister or in the public service. An aspect of his Christianity was his firm, unshakeable belief in the afterlife, and in the reality of the spiritual world. He was sure he got glimpses of it in coincidences, and in his dreams, and he accumulated evidence showing that metaphysical forces were directing his life. He never had a crisis of faith."

"Are you saying," I asked, afraid I might get bad marks in my report at the end of the interview, "that he was already a spiritualist when he went to university?"

"Yes, probably. I do know he became fascinated by spiritualism very early in his life. You know, it was so much more common then than it is now, and entirely respectable."

"But surely he must have been aware of the difference between religion and superstition?"

"I doubt whether that was ever an issue," she said, stroking her double chin. "We are all superstitious, on some level. Besides, belief in spiritual forces strikes me as not categorically different from belief in the subconscious, as determining the way we live. If you like, you can call both exercises in superstition. His main purpose is, and has always been, his idealistic effort to improve himself so that he can improve the lot of others."

I wondered for a moment what Herbert Sloan would have said had he heard this description of his bête noir.

"So when did he start trying to make contact with the spirits in the spiritual world?" I asked, surprised at myself that I could ask this question without flinching.

"Not until quite a long time after the quick succession of the deaths in his family—mother, father, sister—which left him a profoundly lonely bachelor. His brother, Max, had died much earlier. He had never been in good health. His beloved mother, Isabel, died in 1917. These deaths were devastating for him. The only good friend he had ever had, Bert Harper, had died back in 1901, when King was twenty-seven. He wrote a book about him. He did not participate in a séance until 1932, when he was fifty-eight.

"A séance meaning—using a medium, through whom the dead would speak?"

"So I understand."

"But didn't it occur to him that mediums might be unreliable?"

"It most certainly did. For many years he resisted going to a séance, for exactly that reason. But gradually he changed his mind. He read all he could abut psychic research, subscribed to several journals, and was in touch with Professor J.B. Rhine at Duke University, among others, and followed his experiments. And he corresponded with several acquaintances who shared his interests."

"But lately he has done without mediums, I understand. He no longer wants any intermediaries and believes in table rapping. What do you think of that, Miss Surrey? Is that not bound to be fraudulent?"

"Mr. King is academically trained." Her voice was firm. "Even the most sophisticated people in the world believe what they want to believe. Just like you and me. I cannot give you a better answer."

I was now ready to pop the question.

"So, on balance, you think I might as well go ahead?"

"I did not say that. Mr. King has consistently taken the view that this is a private matter. I am not suggesting you should go against his wishes. He knows spiritualism is highly controversial and can easily be misunderstood. But if you do, for your own reasons, you should put it in the right context. Sooner or later it is going to come out anyway."

I was undecided when I went back to Ottawa.

The next day at lunch time, in the cafeteria in the Château, just ahead of me I spotted Pierre Berton. What an amazing coincidence, I thought. The Finger of God. I was just about to go to him and ask whether he had a minute or two to spare for me when I felt a firm hand on my shoulder.

It was my boss, C.D. Howe.

"Could you step aside for a minute, please" he asked in a subdued voice that spelled trouble.

I left the line-up.

"Would you mind coming to see me in my office at three-thirty?" he said in a voice that spelled trouble.

I was there on time. He asked me to sit down.

"I have heard from several sources that you have been giving out financial information to your friends," he said. "You know the rules. You had better look for a new job."

Well, that was that. On the way home I saw Pierre Berton at my street corner. I rushed towards him, but he disappeared in a house before I could reach him.

**Igor Gouzenko:
The Cold War Began in Ottawa**

HENNING ANDERSEN, in his mid forties, looked like an adventurous Danish ship's captain, had a pink face and bright blue eyes, and was immensely likable. I had seen him a few times in a grocery store near the corner of Kent and Somerset where we did our shopping. The Gouzenko family happened to live around the corner, at 511 Somerset. Igor Gouzenko was the young Soviet cipher clerk who made history on September 5, 1945, when he defected, with his pregnant wife and their little boy, Andrei, carrying two hundred and fifty papers with him that documented extensive espionage activities and incriminated thirteen Canadian civil servants and scientists, four probable contacts in the United States and one in Britain.

President Roosevelt had died on April 12, 1945, six months before Gouzenko's defection, and Truman succeeded him. Germany had surrendered on May 7, Japan on August 15. Mackenzie King, age seventy, was prime minister of Canada. In England, exhausted after six years of war, Attlee had succeeded Churchill on July 26. Nominally, the Soviets were still allies of the western powers. but it was not hard to see that the alliance was in serious trouble. Some even feared that there was danger of a third world war, the West against Russia, with Canada as a battleground. One source of tension was the Soviet resentment of the American nuclear monopoly.

"Did I see you walking into the Parliament building?" Henning asked me one day. "Are you a member?"

"Oh no," I laughed and told him I was in Ottawa on a three-month contract, as a researcher for Jean-Luc Desjardins, the parliamentary assistant of the minister of defence.

"I'd like to hear more," he said. "Let me invite you to a pint of beer."

I was delighted especially since it was a hot day. We went to a pub on Bank Street where we had the first of many illuminating conversations.

Henning Andersen was working for Naval Intelligence, which did not prevent him from being a true believer in communism. He was also a passionate opponent of Stalin. Normally he kept his political beliefs secret, but to me, for some reason, he spoke about them freely, though of course in confidence. In spite of his anti-Stalinism he maintained good relations with several members of the Russian embassy, including Igor Gouzenko, before his defection, because Henning had an insatiable curiosity about the way the Soviet mind worked and because he liked Russians.

At the university, idealists were common, but I did not remember ever having met a middle-aged idealist, and certainly not one who was a communist. I had a number of left-wing friends but none of them was radical. I suppose I was mildly left-wing myself, but until I met Henning I had the usual middle-class prejudice against communists. I was, however, hugely impressed by the success of the Red Army and never forgot that the Soviets were our allies. I suspected we would not have won the war in Europe without them. I was even taken to a couple of meetings of the Canadian-Soviet Friendship Council in Toronto, had observed the red flag with hammer and sickle flying above he entrance to Eaton's department store in Montreal to demonstrate the store's devotion to Canadian-Soviet friendship, and was always thrilled when I heard recordings of the Red Army Choir singing *Kalinka, Dark Eyes* and the *Song of the Volga Boatmen.*

"Have you always been a communist, Henning?" I asked him once, a few weeks after that first conversation in the Bank Street pub. By then he had told me about his relations with some of the people in the Soviet embassy and we trusted each other.

"Certainly not," he replied emphatically. "I only became a communist when I learned to think straight. And that was after I had left high school and began travelling—all over Europe, North Africa and South America—and started to read books that I had never seen at home in Copenhagen. My eyes were opened."

"And when did you come to Canada?"

"In 1929. Because of a Montreal girl I had met in Casablanca. It was nice while it lasted... What about you?" he asked.

I told him the essentials. When I had finished I asked him how he had made a living in Montreal. He was a journalist, he said, which was the reason he met all kinds of interesting people. Some of them thought the way he did. And when the Spanish civil war broke out in 1936, he became involved with the North American Committee to Aid Spanish Democracy and made friends with Norman Bethune.

"You knew him?"

I had heard of the courageous doctor who had gone to Spain soon after the outbreak of the civil war and established blood banks that had saved hundreds, maybe thousands of lives.

"I was his assistant," said Henning.

"Really?" I was thrilled to hear it. "Tell me more."

"Well, where do I start? He had two jobs in Montreal. He was a surgeon at the Veterans Hospital and at Sacré Coeur. He was very good at his job, you know, very much in demand, but at the same time he was active politically as a committed anti-fascist. As I was. But unlike me, he was a member of the communist party. Only his close friends knew. Soon after the outbreak of the Spanish civil war he became convinced that this was where the future of the world would be decided, that the fascists would use it as a kind of dress rehearsal. So in October 1936 he resigned from his positions in the two hospitals and left by ship from Quebec City, armed with medical supplies and a letter of introduction to Caballero, the prime minister of Spain. Franco and his nationalist invaders were already threatening Madrid. Before leaving Montreal he had told everybody he would complete his mission whether or not Madrid would fall. When he arrived, Madrid was being bombed. The Germans were trying out their new weapons. I was already there."

"You were?"

"Yes, for the same reasons he was. The committee had asked both of us to report on medical conditions, to let them know what was needed. As you can imagine, it was all rather tense. The militia in Madrid thought we were spies and we were nearly arrested, more than once. Fifth columnists were everywhere. No one was above suspicion.

In the days before Bethune arrived I had done my home work. The two big hotels near the Prado were by now military hospitals. Immediately after Bethune arrived I took him there. After looking things over he decided they had enough surgeons and he could probably be more useful elsewhere. We went to the headquarters of the International Brigade. But this, too, led no where, so we went by train to Valencia. In the train he suddenly said to me, 'Henning, I think I've got an idea.' That's when he told me how to take care of the desperate need for blood transfusions, because of course there was a shortage of blood. It was typical of him that he saw the main problem quickly and found a solution—blood banks. And the rest followed. I was his interpreter, organizer and driver." He paused. "May I now come to the point?"

"The point?"

"Yes, the point. It was in Spain that I learned to detest the Stalinists. They were primarily interested in establishing their own power and influence, and seemed to fight the Trotskyists and anarchists and anybody else who didn't agree with them with as much zest as the fascists. Maybe more. It taught me a lesson I have never forgotten."

"Henning," I asked after a moment while I let this sink in, "what do you say to people who argue that all communists will sooner or later turn into Stalinists?"

I had wondered about that for some time.

"I would say that's absolute nonsense. You are more likely to have freedom of speech and all the other freedoms in a communist society that is not based on exploitation, as is the case in a capitalist society where big business calls the tune."

"But if the state owns all the means of production who can limit its power?"

"When the basic economic questions are solved," he replied, "human beings are free to behave like human beings."

"You mean behave well?"

"Yes," he replied. "And behave badly. It's up to them to choose."

"Is that what you tell your Stalinist friends at the Soviet embassy?" I asked with a smile.

"I haven't as yet, but I will when the right moment comes. I may start at the bottom, or at the top. Who knows? It all depends. I will take my time. By the way, will you come to a reception there on Friday? You will like the free-flowing vodka."

"What a good idea," I exclaimed. "Yes, I would like to very much."

I had been curious to see the inside of the Soviet embassy on Charlotte Street for some time. To do so with Henning as my guide was a truly intriguing prospect.

"You won't notice it, but there's not one person there who wouldn't prefer life in Canada to life at home," he told me. "You can't imagine the contrast—Russia was devastated by the war. The Russians have—*nothing*. For them life in Canada is sheer heaven. That's why their parties are so good—they are happy to be here. If they had a chance, they would all stay. But they can't say so. They can't even whisper this to each other. The very suggestion is high treason and means Siberia. They're all terrified to be betrayed to their bosses."

So on August 12 we went. It was a Soviet holiday, an anniversary of something or other. We saw quite a number of high-level Canadians, and people from other embassies. And many lovely women. There was a sumptuous buffet with all kinds of delicacies, including caviar, and live music performed by men in uniform playing the harmonica and some sort of plucked instrument. We shook hands with the ambassador, Georgi Zarubin, and his handsome wife. We met the military attaché, Colonel Nikolai Zabotin, who was also—the Canadian authorities did not yet know that—in charge of GRU operations, i.e., espionage in Canada. I soon learned he was a veteran of the battle of Stalingrad and the son of a tsarist officer. He was said to have seduced at least two diplomatic wives, maybe more. We also talked to the consul, Vitaliy Pavlov, impressive with high cheekbones, like a Hollywood Russian. It was not surprising that capitalist Ottawa hostesses were vying with each other to have a decorative Soviet official at their dinner parties. We also met a man from the National Film Board who had produced *Our Northern Neighbour.*

And then there was the subject of this story—the young cipher clerk Igor Gouzenko and his attractive wife, Anna, three weeks before their defection. He had a high forehead and unusually heavy eyebrows, was serious minded and intelligent. He did not smile much and, on the whole, lacked charm. He spoke enough English to be able to converse with us, unlike Anna, who knew no English at all.

"How are you getting on with your new bicycle?" Henning asked.

"Better than the one I had at home," Gouzenko replied.

That was not yet high treason, and no indication of the things to come. But Henning told me later that he had the impression from previous conversations with Gouzenko that he was a candidate for defection. He thought he would perform an invaluable service to his anti-Stalinist cause if he followed up this intuition by suggesting to him as subtly as possible that such a step was—let us say—conceivable. He could not have known that Gouzenko, with his wife's whole-hearted concurrence, was already considering defection. They preferred to bring up their children in capitalist comfort rather than in Stalin's sordid Russia. However, they knew what dangers they faced and had to think things through first with the utmost care.

They were very much aware of the danger that he could be recalled at any moment, for one reason or another, and they had to be ready to act should this happen. They knew that Zabotin's assistant, Major Alexander Romanov, like his boss a veteran of Stalingrad, had been sent back to Moscow ignominiously a few weeks earlier because of episodes of drunken and disorderly conduct including "inappropriate"—so it said in the reports—advances to the wife of a general in the Canadian army. (What would be "appropriate" advances?) Gouzenko was determined not to follow suit. They assumed Romanov was by now in a labour camp in Siberia. (That is how Romanov's boss, the lady-killer Zabotin, was punished a few months later for not being able to prevent Gouzenko's defection. He was not released until 1953.)

A week before the reception Henning had gone so far as to mention to Gouzenko the name of Victor Kravchenko, the author of *I Chose Freedom,* who had defected a year earlier in the U.S. and had been granted asylum by Roosevelt. Gouzenko knew all about him. But, strangely enough, this did not indicate to Henning that Gouzenko was already playing with the idea of following Kravchenko's example. He was clearly a master at dissembling and Henning was uncharacteristically tone-deaf at that moment. Gouzenko told him later that he had been warned in Moscow, before he left, that cipher clerks were obvious targets by counter-intelligence agents who might make him all kinds of tempting offers, knowing that cipher clerks were storehouses of secret information. Perhaps that remark, too—especially the word *tempting*—should have given a hint to Henning, but it did not.

Gouzenko was right to worry. Just as he feared, he discovered two days after the reception that he had fallen into disfavour for a number of far less interesting reasons than Romanov's. He had left scraps of paper with secret information on the floor of the cipher room, where they were discovered by a cleaning lady who handed them to embassy officials. He had been seen talking to Ottawa policemen, which was considered a serious offence. He had been late for work on several occasions and been reprimanded. But, far more important, he had displeased Colonel Mikhail Milshtein, a highly placed official in NKVD, the People's Commissariat for Internal Affairs in Moscow, who had been suspicious of him from the start. Milshtein had discovered that Gouzenko had unauthorized access to a safe in the cipher room.

It was now clear to Gouzenko that at any moment he would be recalled. Therefore, on the hot and sultry evening of Wednesday, September 5, 1945, he, pregnant Anna and little Andrei took the fateful step.

We did not find out what happened to them after that step until the hearings of the Kellock-Taschereau royal commission, which was appointed on February 5, 1946, to investigate the affair. Only then, five months after the event, did the affair become known all over the world. Until then all we knew was what Henning had found out about it two days after the defection, when he went to see his friends at the Soviet embassy as he had done many times before. Not only did he find Gouzenko missing, but everybody froze when he mentioned his name. This time Henning was not tone-deaf. He knew immediately what had happened. After his visit he called a contact at the RCMP, who confirmed the defection on condition of absolute secrecy. But he would not say anything more.

On March 5, six months after the defection, Churchill made his famous speech in Fulton, Missouri, declaring, in the presence of President Truman, that an iron curtain had descended across Europe. The Canadian ambassador in Washington, Lester Pearson, had seen the text in advance and approved it. One reason for the speech was the Gouzenko affair.

Three weeks before the speech, on February 15, thirteen Canadian suspects were arrested and Gouzenko made headlines all over the world. By then he and his family were solidly ensconced in RCMP custody, inaccessible. It had become clear that the information the Soviets had attempted to obtain through espionage was above all connected with the building of an atomic bomb. It had taken the governments and intelligence services of Canada, the United Kingdom and the United States five months to reach an agreement on how to proceed with the minimum of damage to diplomatic relations with the USSR.

The hearings of the Kellock-Taschereau commission did not only shake the world but also—as will become clear—shook Henning personally in a way no one could have predicted.

But first I must relate what happened after Gouzenko— almost paralyzed with fear—left the embassy, equipped with two hundred and fifty secret documents—among them Soviet code books and deciphering material, whether in a cardboard box or in one or two briefcases—that is not clear. Anna and Andrei were in their apartment on Somerset.

Kravchenko had gone to the *New York Times*. So Gouzenko went to the *Ottawa Journal*. The night editor on duty recalled that Gouzenko was so agitated that he was unable to answer any of his questions, and just stood there and repeated "It's war. It's Russia." An eyewitness later remarked that "nobody could figure out what the hell the guy wanted." The editor suggested he go to the RCMP offices, which were in the building of the Minister of Justice, not far from the *Journal*'s offices. Gouzenko went there and asked the policeman at the door to see Louis St. Laurent, the minister of justice, not the RCMP. He was in such a frenzy, he was obviously not thinking straight. Naturally he was told to come back in the morning. He returned home to a frantic Anna. Then, with Andrei in tow, he went back to the *Journal*, still incoherent. Since his story was unsubstantiated and could damage Canadian-Soviet relations, the editors decided they could not run it. They suggested he go to the RCMP's Bureau of Naturalization. He did, asked for protection and was refused. He tried other approaches and was equally unsuccessful. By then Andrei was getting tired and hungry. The Gouzenkos were besides themselves with fear for their lives; Igor's absence and the missing documents must by now have been noticed by the embassy.

He appealed to a neighbour to take them in. Around midnight men from the embassy led by the NKVD's Vitaliy Pavlov arrived, broke into the apartment and ransacked it, looking for the stolen documents, until the police arrived. Gouzenko watched the scene, peering through the neighbour's keyhole across the hall.

All this happened around the corner from where I lived—but I heard nothing.

The next morning the Gouzenkos were escorted to the RCMP. At last they were safe.

But this is not where my story ends.

The Kellock-Taschereau commission hearings were an international media event. On February 20 the Soviet government admitted spying in Canada. On that day my jaw dropped when I read in the papers that one of the documents Gouzenko had smuggled out of the embassy was a notebook of Colonel Zabotin's containing dozens of contacts, one of which was:

> H. Andrason. In Naval Department. Works in Intelligence. Use to give material on construction of ships.

Andrason, not Andersen. Still—is it conceivable—I simply could not help asking myself the disloyal question—that Henning ... ? That he deceived me to protect himself, that in spite of the frequent anti-Stalinist talk he was after all more of a communist than an anti-Stalinist, and that he was actually a Soviet spy? And that this was the reason why he was such a welcome guest at the Soviet embassy?

I need not have worried. Before I had a chance to call him he called me.

"I know what you're thinking," he said, laughing. "I would be thinking the same thing if I was in your shoes. No need to deny it."

I don't remember what I stuttered.

"I've been in touch with the commission. They have agreed to take my testimony. I will clear my name. You will see: they will believe me. This is not the Soviet Union."

And that is exactly what happened. He told the commission that in 1937 he served as a liaison officer in Spain between Norman Bethune's hospital group and the Spanish Republican Army, that in January 1938 he returned to Canada, that in April 1940 he became naturalized and that he then spent two years in South America, returning to Canada in November 1942. He applied at once to join the Navy, receiving his commission in November 1943. By then he had declared to the naval authorities, and to the RCMP, that he remained a communist but that he was committed to fighting the Nazis, and that, after all, the USSR was Canada's ally.

In a sharp exchange with the commission's lawyers he declared his unqualified loyalty to Canada, and convinced them that, just as he had not been a security risk during the war, he was not one now. His political beliefs were a private matter that would not in any way influence his behaviour as a Canadian citizen and naval officer.

The commission accepted his testimony. The entry in Zabotin's notebook was never explained.

In 1962 Henning went to Fidel Castro's Cuba and became a high-level advisor to the government. To judge from his annual Christmas cards, he was very happy there—until he died in 1985.

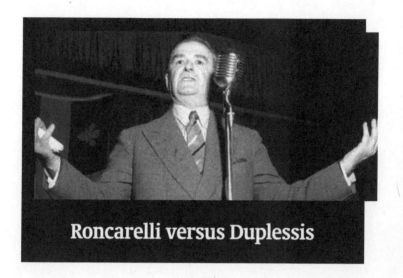

Roncarelli versus Duplessis

SHEILA BLANDFORD was aghast when Frank Roncarelli told her he was going to fight for the Jehovah's Witnesses.

"Why would you do such a thing?" she asked.

"They need me. It's as simple as that."

"But they are so *uncouth*," she exclaimed. "And they talk such *drivel*."

"One has to learn not to listen."

Sheila had told him the moment she found out he was involved with the sect that she was appalled. She knew it had little to do with religion. He had other reasons.

The time was late October 1946, the place the front room in Sheila's haute couture dress shop on Sherbrooke Street in Montreal, near the corner of Crescent Street.

Sheila had arrived in Canada from England in 1935. She was good looking, brisk and business-like, and she spoke perfect French, which she had learned at a finishing school in Switzerland. But, as it happened, she did not need it in Montreal since most of her wealthy customers lived in English-speaking Westmount. She was now pondering whether to take the adventurous step to open a second shop in Quebec City, a different world. She liked the French in Europe and the French in Canada.

For six years after September 1939 Sheila spent nearly half her time doing war work for the Red Cross.

Frank was born in Italy and came over with his family when he was five. An engineer by training, he had made a great deal of money in highway construction. But he got tired of it and found it more satisfying to be the owner of the excellent Italian restaurant at 1429 Crescent, not far from Sheila's shop, just north of St. Catherine Street. His father had run it for thirty-four years. That is where he met Sheila during the war.

They were an incongruous couple. Both were articulate and enterprising and in spite of—or perhaps because of—the difference in their backgrounds they enjoyed each other's company enormously. Frank's generous wife did not seem to mind, and Sheila had managed to avoid marriage so far.

Frank was a lapsed Catholic. Religion played no role in his life until he became aware of the persecution of Jehovah's Witnesses by the premier of Quebec, Maurice Duplessis. That awareness had to do with political morality rather than with religion.

The sect had been conducting a successful campaign proselytizing Catholics. Its members believed there should be no mediating agency between the individual and God and were therefore the enemies of all churches. Quebec was eighty-five percent Catholic.

Duplessis's Padlock Law, passed in 1937 was designed to prevent the dissemination of communist propaganda. He now declared a "war without mercy" on the Jehovah's Witnesses. The municipality of Montreal had on its books a number of by-laws that could easily be made to serve the same purpose.

Frank's lifestyle was more North American than Québécois, let alone Italian, and he identified himself with the non-Catholic communities in Montreal. But even if that had not been the case, Duplessis' repression deeply offended his sense of justice, as it did that of a number of tolerant French Canadians.

As the Montreal police began to arrest Witnesses for harassing people on the street to sell copies of *The Watch-Tower* and *Awake* and canvassing from door to door, Frank proceeded to post bail for the victims. By November 21, 1946, he had done so three hundred and ninety three times. On that day Duplessis publicly warned him that if he did not stop interfering with the administration of justice he would lose his restaurant's liquor licence.

The next day Frank took Sheila to see Jean-Paul Sartre's play *No Exit* at the Montreal Repertory Theatre on Guy Street. Afterwards, while walking up Côtes des Neiges towards Sheila's apartment, he told her he would ignore Duplessis's warning.

She was not pleased to hear it.

"He will do everything he can to ruin you," Sheila warned him. "And he's bigger than you are."

"He used to be," Frank replied. "Times have changed. Autocrats are no longer as big as they once were. It makes no sense to me to give in, Sheila. We didn't give in when Hitler and Mussolini went on a rampage, and look where they are now."

Sheila sighed. "I don't want to sound like Chamberlain, but what about using a little diplomacy first?"

"I'll leave that to you, my dear."

"I know you think I am a snob," Sheila said, "but I can't help wishing you would fight for people with whom you have more in common."

"Too bad one can't pick and choose one's battles. As we have just learned in Sartre's play, hell is other people. One cannot fight them all."

"How very true," she agreed with a wry smile. "You go ahead and do what you think right, and I will go to Quebec City to the lion's den and see what I can do. As you know, I was going to go there anyway."

They had often discussed the possibilities of a second store in the province's capital.

"Remember Chamberlain," he said.

On December 4, Édouard Archambault, the chair of the Quebec Liquor Commission, denied the renewal of Frank's liquor licence. It was not hard to guess that the action was inspired by Duplessis, who was attorney general in addition to being premier. The police seized about $2,000 worth of alcoholic beverages. This unleashed a storm of protest in the English community. On December 12, a meeting was held at the Monument-National on Bleary Street, but it was less than successful. No celebrities spoke and there was a good deal of grandiloquent name calling—Duplessis was called a Nazi and a Fascist—but the press paid little attention. As Sheila had feared, the Jehovah's Witnesses had antagonized too many people, among others the Protestant clergy who could not in any case get very excited about a man's right to sell, of all things, liquor. Frank's cause was obviously not popular. The protest fizzled out.

On the train to Quebec City Sheila tried to figure out what her strategy should be. She had no illusions. She knew her chances were remote. Her friends were mainly in the fashion business and, of course, she had no experience in political lobbying. However, if anybody could help her it was a man who had nothing whatever to do with the fashion business. It was her worldly-wise Austrian friend Karl von Schwarzenfeld, a distant relative of the Habsburgs, whom she had met at a party in the Park Lane Hotel in Piccadilly when she was on vacation in London in the spring of 1938.

Karl was a small round-faced bachelor whose amusing party talk was carefully designed to conceal that he was not really an effete aristocrat, a role he admittedly enjoyed playing, but a serious, versatile and public-spirited man of conscience. She liked him the moment she met him, and this sentiment was obviously mutual.

Karl had just arrived as a refugee from Vienna, after the Nazi annexation of Austria. As a result of understandable panic in May 1940 he was interned as an "enemy alien," although he was a committed and courageous anti-Nazi. With many others he was shipped to Canada, spent the summer of 1940 in a camp on the historic Plains of Abraham in the centre of Quebec City, the very site of the battlefield where the English wrestled Canada from the French in 1763. The camp had a stunning view of the St. Lawrence valley, and because of the views—so Karl said— he chose Quebec City as his Canadian residence after his release a year and a half later. He had been a passionate amateur cook and baker in Vienna, where members of the old nobility often indulged themselves in odd hobbies if they could still afford them, and he was much sought after by hostesses with good taste, who gave him the opportunity to display his skills in the kitchen before being invited to join the party. So he was delighted to accept the job of pastry chef in the imposing Château Frontenac hotel, the epicentre of political Quebec and residence of

Maurice Duplessis. He was invariably the first customer in the barbershop on the ground floor, at 6:30 a.m. Before accepting the job, Karl had (temporarily) dropped the *von* from his name.

The trick was to persuade Duplessis that it was in his interest to restore Frank's licence in return for some kind of undertaking by the Witnesses that they would mend their ways. Their campaign was sooner or later going to wind down anyway. Sheila was confident that she could persuade Frank to use his influence to sway them.

As soon as she had checked into the small, exclusive Lamartine Hotel on a little street off the Grande Allée, she called Karl and invited him to a drink in the bar at six.

When he came, she ordered martinis and told him about her mission.

"Oh dear, oh dear, oh dear," he said, stroking his prominent chin. "This requires the talents of Machiavelli, Talleyrand and Bismarck combined. All the cards are in Duplessis's hands. No one likes the Witnesses. Except three former monks they converted and who are now helping me make *méringues* in my kitchen. They are as outraged by his statement as I am."

"What statement?"

Karl found a newspaper on a table nearby and began reading:

> To have permitted Frank Roncarelli, self-styled leader of the Witnesses, to continue the use of funds derived from a privilege granted him by the Province of Quebec to conduct a campaign inciting to sedition, public disorder and disregard for municipal by-laws would have been

to put the attorney general of the province in the position of an accomplice. The fact that a man posts bail for a friend or two is quite in order, but when a man creates an organization for masses of people who are jointly engaged in law-breaking, it becomes a different matter.

"By that logic," Sheila observed quietly, "the City of Montreal is an accomplice because it gives him water, the Quebec Hydro because it gives him electricity, and the Bell because it provides him with a telephone. Why don't you say that to Duplessis when he drops in on you in your kitchen?"

"He does not visit the lower depths," said Karl, laughing. "I have never spoken a word to him in my life. Which may be a pity because my spies tell me he is a perfectly nice, amusing character when he is not a politician. But they also tell me his mood has deteriorated noticeably since he had to give up drinking. For reasons of health. Maybe we should engage his doctor and have him explain to him that the purpose of bail is the precise opposite of what he says. It *helps* the administration of justice. It is designed to make sure the accused persons appear in court. The precise opposite of inciting sedition and public disorder."

"Who can tell him that?" Sheila asked.

"Oh, he knows it perfectly well," Karl replied. "He is a lawyer. His favourite literature is law books. Although he boasts that he never reads a book. He knows there is nothing illegal about Roncarelli putting spokes in the wheel of his war against the Witnesses. Defending Catholic Quebec against trouble makers whom everybody regards as a public nuisance is all that matters."

Sheila ordered another martini and sighed. "What on earth should we do, Karl?"

"Simple. We have to convince him that he will lose important friends unless he restores Roncarelli's licence. I mean his friends on St. James Street in Montreal—big money, capitalists, the people for whom he has been bullying the labour bosses and fighting the unions, for whom he has bartered away for a pittance the Hollinger mining company, probably containing the richest iron ore on the continent. He is a modernizer, he believes in industrialization and he assumes that is the way to preserve the old Quebec."

"What a pipedream." Sheila took a sip of her second martini. "So you think Duplessis can be made to listen to reason?"'

"We won't know until we try," Karl replied. "Somebody has to tell him that St. James Street does not like arbitrary acts. To them it means mob rule. The rich prefer the rule of law. Nothing else makes them feel safe."

"Good thinking, Karl."

Unfortunately, the thinking was not good enough. Sheila's diplomacy failed.

Frank, not Sheila, turned out to be the giant killer. But it took him thirteen years. Overcoming setback after setback he sued Duplessis personally, and with the help of F.R. Scott, the brilliant dean of the McGill law school and a noted poet, took the matter right up to the Supreme Court. They won, in a landmark decision. Duplessis had to pay $33,123.53 in damages. Judgment was passed on January 27, 1959.

On September 7, 1959, Duplessis died.

By then Frank had moved to Connecticut and resumed

his career as an engineer in highway construction.

And Sheila was happily married to Karl von Schwarzenfeld.

Camillien Houde:
The Cyrano of Montreal

When I told my well-connected father that I was down and out once again, he had a bright idea. A friend of his who was close to the Montreal City Council had told him a few days ago that Mayor Camillien Houde intended to give a reception in the ballroom of the Windsor Hotel to convey to English Montreal that he had forgiven Ottawa for keeping him behind barbed wire for four years during the war. It was clear to my father's friend that Houde needed an expert to help his staff prepare a guest list. Houde knew who was who on the French side, but the English were often a puzzle to him. Who was more qualified for this delicate task than a young man whose social agility had become legendary?

Of course I was delighted to accept. I knew the basic facts. Six years ago, on August 2, 1940, eleven months after the war had broken out, the flamboyant and hugely popular mayor spoke informally to a group of reporters, including Campbell Carroll of the Gazette, and told them he was not going to obey the Defence of Canada regulations demanding that all Canadians over the age of sixteen register for possible war service.

To Houde, and to many others, registration meant a step towards conscription. In 1917, during the First World

War, conscription had divided the country. This time, once again, many French Canadians were not willing to fight "for the English king." Carroll immediately recognized that Houde had committed an act of sedition, if not high treason, and phoned his editor, Tracy Ludington, to tell him. Ludington asked Carroll to type out a statement and ask Houde to sign it. Houde did so with a cheerful flourish. That evening the first edition of the Gazette was on the street, with the story on the front page. Within an hour the government censor phoned Ludington demanding that the newspaper drop this incitement to civil disobedience from the next edition. The following day Robert Hanson, the leader of the opposition in Ottawa, brought up the matter in the House of Commons. Now the story was out and made headlines all over the country, including the Gazette. Three days later, on August fifth, an RCMP squad arrested Houde in the city hall. He was taken away by car. According to regulations, he was not told where he was being taken, and he kept asking, "Where are you taking me?" He received no reply. Over the following four years of incarceration in an internment camp in Petawawa, near Ottawa, and later in another camp in Minto near Fredericton, New Brunswick, he was told repeatedly he would be released if he recanted. He refused to do so.

One of the charms of my new assignment was that it might help me discover whether, in 1940, Houde knew what he was doing when he so brazenly defied the law. Did he really think that Prime Minister Mackenzie King would not dare to touch him, "le chum de tout le monde," as the historian Robert Rumilly called him? I remembered that the French Canadian press was by no means enchanted with the mayor. No doubt many who admired him for the position he had taken kept it to themselves. La Presse wrote that all law-abiding French Canadians were shocked by Houde's defiance, and Le Devoir said he had acted like a fool and had got what he deserved. Cardinal Villeneuve urged Catholics to comply with the law. Most French Canadians registered without any fuss and carried their registration certificates obediently in their wallets for the rest of the war.

So why was Houde so reckless? Did he think that in the end he would turn out to be the winner after all and perhaps even supplant Maurice Duplessis, premier of Quebec, the man who in 1932 had ousted him as leader of the provincial Conservatives?

This was my chance to find out.

On August 16, 1944, after 1,472 days of incarceration, when the allies were clearly winning the war and Houde was no longer considered a danger, he was released and welcomed home by ten thousand flower-throwing enthusiasts at Central Station singing "Il a gagné ses épaulettes." In December—still before the war was over—he was re-elected mayor with a wide margin.

A year and a half later, in August 1946, I entered the picture when he received me in his office to give me my instructions. I had only seen him in newsreels and photographs, so I knew what he looked like: fat, with a big bulbous nose and quick, shrewd eyes. I remembered that allegedly at a school theatrical he had acted Cyrano de Bergerac without having had to put on a putty nose.

He greeted me in English but I thought it would be diplomatic to respond in French.

"No, no, no, monsieur, " he stopped me. "I must practise my English. I worked hard on it in the camps. Did you know I did not know a word of English until I was twenty-five?"

"No, Your Worship," I replied. "I did not know that. All I know is that in the internment camp you were the Chinese checkers champion."

"So you have done your homework." His double chin shook as he laughed. "Very promising. So you are going to help me. Excellent." His English was remarkably good, but occasionally he had to search for the right word.

"My staff has already prepared a list. I want about a hundred anglos." He swallowed hard. "I know you're also an anglo, but you're not a Montreal anglo. But I'm told you know them well. I am fully aware that few of them like me. At my last election I understand some of them who were in hospitals even insisted on being taken to the polling stations in stretchers to vote against me. But I say 'Never mind, forgiveness is in the air.' The fine people who arranged the St. Andrew's Ball even invited me to dance with them, the first anglo ball after the war. I borrowed a kilt and went. I told them I was Scottish, and Houde was really Howe, and I was a cousin of C.D. Howe. That got me a good laugh. I even forgive the Gazette for getting me interned. Although quite recently they said the nastiest things about me. But nevertheless their editor Charles Peters"—he pronounced the name in English—"and invited me to dinner at the Windsor Hotel to tell me it was time to turn the page." He swallowed hard. "I accepted, on condition that he get a table in the centre of the big dining room to make sure that everybody could see us together. The war is over and done with and we have to think ahead. Please look over our list, correct it and make any suggestions you like. Is that okay with you?"

I told him I would do my best. On the way out a secretary handed me a blue file labeled "Anglos." I took it home and studied it. Houde's staff had done an impressive job but there were some serious gaps. Nobody from the Protestant school board was invited. Nor was any Protestant clergyman or rabbi. But the popular hosts from private radio stations, CJAD and CKAC, were on the list, and so was Rupert Caplan, Montreal's CBC drama producer. McGill and Concordia universities were well represented. But they hadn't thought of Mary Winspear, the headmistress of Weston School, a private school for girls, who was a friend of my father and whom I had known since I was a little boy. She certainly was a member of the anglo elite, well known in the community for her wide interests and social conscience. Nor had they thought of Harold Dingman, the journalist who did not speak a word of French and who had said, after he had heard Houde speak at some banquet or other, "I didn't understand a word he said, but he sure convinced me." And they had not thought of the novelist Hugh MacLennan. And, of course, it would be a coup to persuade Colonel R.P. Rutherford to come, the Montreal lawyer who had taken time off to serve as the commandant of the Petawawa internment camp. He would have many interesting things to say about Houde in captivity. But would he accept? I had better go to see him and find out. For that matter, I should not suggest any of these people unless I first sounded them out.

So I went to see Mary Winspear, the imposing, worldly principal of the school on Severn Avenue in Westmount. As a child I would call her "Aunt Mary."

"So you got yourself a nice little job, my boy," she greeted me, with her crisp British accent. "Forgiveness is always a good cause."

"As long as one doesn't go too far," I observed, with my usual sense of prudent moderation.

"I can't disagree with that," she laughed. "I don't really approve of sedition and high treason. And I won't make any excuses for the old trouble maker. I was told years ago that he kept a photograph of Mussolini at his bedside, and that he believed all French Canadians were Latins at heart and were inclined towards fascism. That absurd opinion, of course, was not what got him interned, far from it. Still, if I had the choice between spending an evening with Mackenzie King or with Camillien Houde, I would choose Houde any time. I prefer lovable rogues to constipated puritans."

"You'll have your chance in the Windsor Hotel."

"I am looking forward to it. Mackenzie King never invited me to anything. And I am perfectly happy to give Houde credit for the tremendous job he did in the Depression, even if he did bankrupt the city. By the time he was through, our city debt was ten times that of Toronto's. As you know, Montreal had to be put into trusteeship, and he was left in his office merely as a figurehead. Which is what he is now. Having been poor himself, he couldn't bear the suffering of so many, and he put thousands of people to work creating the farmers' markets at Jean Talon, St. James and Atwater, and the Botanical Gardens and the Lookout, and the chalet on top of the mountain, and St. Helen's Island, and, above all, the Camiliennes, the public toilets, that sprinkle the city. For this he has earned the eternal gratitude of one and all. Once, when he was asked whether he would build more urinals in the city, he replied, 'not only urinals, but also arsenals.' No wonder everybody loved him. He has a heart of pure gold." She paused. Then she remembered another story. "One day, a delegation of the poor called on him asking for relief. He gave them his month's salary. That evening he had dinner at the Traymore restaurant. He had forgotten he had given all his money away, so he had to phone a friend to rescue him."

"What do you know about his childhood?"

"One of our more enterprising history teachers gave an assignment to her senior class to write a paper about it. The students had some trouble uncovering the sources but what they found was eye-opening. He was born in 1889 on the rue St. Martin, in the poorest part of St. Henri in a two-room tenement flat. He was the oldest of ten children who all died before they were two. The father had a small job in a flour mill and died when Camillien was nine. The mother, Joséphine, became a dressmaker. Camillien made a dollar a week as a part-time butcher's boy and occasionally brought home a piece of meat for dinner. Joséphine allowed him to keep five cents a week for pocket money. She saved the rest for his education. He completed a commercial course when he was sixteen and got a job as a clerk at the Bank of Hochelaga. He stayed at the bank and became branch manager at twenty-six. At thirty-three he was earning only forty dollars a week. One day, he went to a fortune teller who read his hand. She saw him 'talking triumphantly at street corners and shaking hands.' He had been interested in politics anyway. So he joined the Conservative Party. It was so unpopular in Quebec so he had no trouble being nominated. He ran in a provincial election in the Ste. Marie riding and won. That was his beginning in politics. He soon noticed that he was a born orator, that he could rouse people to indignation, laughter and tears with no effort at all. That gave him tremendous self-confidence. You probably know how he managed the ups and downs of the rest of his climb upwards so I won't bore you with the details. In business he tried everything, He was an insurance agent, a biscuit merchant, a candy manufacturer and an importer of wines, and Heaven knows what else. I'll be happy to forgive him for his many sins and come to the reception."

My next chore was to sound out Harold Dingman, whom I had never met before. I found him in shirt sleeves at his office at The Herald.

"That's a terrible idea," he said. "If I'm on the guest list I have to be polite to my host when I write about the event. I'd much cover it as a reporter."

"If the press is invited."

"If it isn't, I'll talk to the guests afterwards. I'm not really the forgive-and-forget type. I think what he did was atrocious. He didn't tell the king that he was not going to fight for him, back in June 1939."

Dingman was referring to the time of the Royal Tour when the king and queen came to Canada. War with Germany was in the air and England wanted to make sure Canada would be onside. The newspaper man leaned back in his chair and smiled.

"That tour gave Camillien Houde what Churchill would have called his 'finest hour.' He loved every moment he was in the royal presence, especially during the highlight of the tour, the glittering state banquet in the Windsor Hotel. Do you know the two stories that circulated about that historic banquet?"

"No," I said.

"Well, instead of eating his sorbet au curaçao, so the first story goes, he was studying a piece of paper. King George VI finally asked him what he was reading. 'Forgive me, Your Majesty,' Houde replied, 'but I have been trying to memorize the list given to me by my advisors who do not trust my judgement of forbidden topics that under no circumstances I was to bring up.' He then handed the list to the king, who startled their fellow guests with his loud laughter. At the end of the speech making, Houde said, 'I thank you from the bottom of my heart for coming. And my wife thanks you from her bottom, too.' After the royal couple returned to England the queen was supposed to have said Camillien Houde was by far the most interesting person they had met in Canada.

"And what was the other story?"

"Oh yes. When the tour arrived at the City Hall, and hundreds of children cheered and sang 'God save the King' and 'Dieu sauve le Roi,' Houde turned to the king and said, 'You know, Your Majesty, some of these cheers are for you also.'—Oh, by the way, did any of the Protestant clergy accept?"

"As a matter of fact," I replied. "None were on the list."

"I am not surprised," Dingman said. "Houde's people know better than to invite them. None of them would accept. And this has nothing to do with the reasons for the internment."

"What do you mean?"

"I mean Houde is anathema to them. He seems to have no objections whatsoever to the Red Light District along the lower reaches of St. Lawrence Boulevard. On the contrary, he probably thinks that's what makes his city great. Catholics are more realistic and tolerant about these matters than Protestants."

"Is there any evidence that he ever said that?"

"Of course not. I am only putting two and two together. He must know perfectly well that the madams pay off the police, and he does nothing to stop it. So naturally the Protestant clergy would stay away, and they know it. But please don't misunderstand me." Dingman laughed. "That's certainly not the reason why I prefer not to be invited."

The next name on my list was Colonel Rutherford, the former commandant at Petawawa. It had taken me some time to dig up his name, and I knew my chances were not good. I was right.

He was a man in his late sixties with a deeply lined face who had fought in World War One. He received me in his law office on St. James Street and was barely polite.

"I am not prepared to give Houde that pleasure," he said after I had made my case. "He wants to say let bygones be bygones. Well, I will not, not after what he has done. He also wants to turn the tables. He wants me to bow to him. That is absolutely out of the question. Young man, you are wasting your time."

I had to put the record straight.

"Sir, coming to see you was my idea, not his."

"A misguided idea, if I may say so, whoever thought of it. I never had anything to do with the man when he was in my camp. I left that to my sergeant-major. I was never sorry for him, not for a second. I was told he had absolutely no awareness of the nature and consequences of what he had done. He insisted the law was on his side, because he was incarcerated without a trial. He was adamant about that. Well, that was crazy. He played the innocent victim. He knew better. Being a politician through and through, he probably thought his defiance would pay off, sooner or later. Disgusting. He could have been released any time if he had changed his mind. His wife wrote him letters addressed to the 'héro prisonnier Camillien Houde.' Some hero! For me he was Prisoner 694, that's all. I had far more sympathy with the Italian waiters who had never bothered to get themselves naturalized and were interned as enemy aliens because years ago they had been talked into joining a fascist organization on the assumption that it was some sort of patriotic club and that they owed it to their grandmothers."

"What, sir, did your sergeant-major report to you about Houde's conduct?"

"That it was impeccable. Houde observed all the rules and regulations punctiliously, without ever making a fuss. He even made his bed the correct way. He was everybody's friend and shared the delicacies his wife sent him with everybody. Naturally he was elected leader of his hut. He got on well with the communists and the fascists. He told the sergeant-major he preferred the communists to the fascists because they had a sense of humour. I never detected that in the dealings I had with communists, I must say. Not that I prefer the fascists."

He picked a paper from his desk, indicating that the interview was over. I thanked him and left.

The last person to sound out was the writer Hugh MacLennan, an English teacher at Lower Canada College on Royal Avenue in Notre Dame de Grâce, the Montreal equivalent of Toronto's prestigious Upper Canada College. I had not read his recent novel, Two Solitudes, which I was told dealt with English-French relations in Canada. That is why I thought—as it turned out, correctly—it would be a good idea to invite him.

He was a handsome man of about forty who had been born in Nova Scotia and lived in Montreal for only eight years. Therefore he could look at the Houde phenomenon with an observer's analytical detachment.

"Yes," MacLennan said. "I would be delighted to come. It's most important that people like me rub shoulders with people like him."

He spoke slowly, as though he was reading a script he had prepared. One could hear that he came from the Maritimes but one could also detect that he had been at Oxford.

"Houde is an extraordinary man. No public figure has ever equalled him in his capacity to express Montreal's spirit of wit, tolerance, perversity, cynicism, gaiety, bawdiness, gallantry, delight in living and—make no mistake about this—dignity."

I could see that the boys at Lower Canada College were lucky to have MacLennan as an English teacher.

"On the drab stage of Canadian public life," he went on, "Houde moves with a grotesque panache, a bizarre poetry, a colossal appetite for life. But—and this is what makes his case so unusual—he is by no means typical. Not many French Canadians have sympathy with the position he took in 1940. Most of them understood that England's case was also their case and the case of humanity as whole. Houde belonged to a small group of trouble makers who wanted to resist the war altogether. That was not the true spirit of Quebec. At the same time, it is neither fair nor sensible for anyone to expect French-speaking Canadians to feel it necessary to fight merely because Great Britain happens to be at war. There will never be a Canadian national understanding until that fact is accepted and respected."

"I agree entirely," I said. "There seems to be a lot of confusion on this point."

"Absolutely. I'd be happy to clarify it to anybody at the reception if I am invited. Montreal is the crucible of Canada's national future. What is wrong in this city is what is wrong in the country itself—the non-understanding between the English and the French."

"One wonders what is worse," I said, "non-understanding or misunderstanding."

"Non-understanding. Misunderstandings can often be cleared up in a minute with a word of two, but non-understanding may require generations. Four years ago I wrote a piece I called 'Culture, Canadian Style.' I came to the conclusion that if Canada was to have a national literature at all, it had better become a nation first. This seemed quite remote since loyalty to a region almost invariably superseded loyalty to the country. This was due to the universal Canadian trait of caution. This caution is born of the experience of failure that each of the three founding groups had experienced in the past, the French, the United Empire Loyalists and the Scottish. Before we can have a national consciousness the descendants of these three groups must stop thinking about themselves as losers and pull together towards a greater destiny. And the place to start this process is clearly Montreal, where all of us with our memories of loss live side by side without—so far—coming together. And the person to bring us together may well be Camillien Houde, who has worked so hard to overcome his own losses and, in his endearing, shrewd, bizarre and humorous way, may well show us the way towards a—dare I say it?—memorable future. Yes, I will come if I am invited."

Hugh MacLennan had chosen his words well. Shrewd was right.

Camillien Houde understood that his defiance of the law in 1940 and subsequent incarceration would, in the end, work to his advantage. Every year since his release he sent a Christmas present to Tracy Ludington, the city editor of the Gazette, the man who started him on the road to internment. Houde was infinitely grateful to him for having made him a martyr.

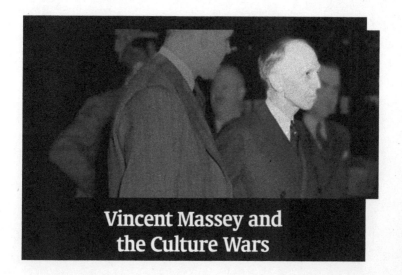

Vincent Massey and
the Culture Wars

THIS TURNED OUT TO BE one of the pleasantest—and easiest—jobs I ever had. It was pure joy, from the very beginning when Archie Day, the secretary of the Massey Commission—Vincent Massey, the future governor general, was the chairman—called me to ask whether I would like to do "a little trouble shooting" for them, to the happy end.

I had met Archie a few times at parties in Ottawa. He had been a professor of classics at the University of Toronto, at McMaster and at Queen's universities. but moved on to External Affairs and was now, in April 1950, on loan to the commission. I had been told that it was Lester Pearson, the secretary of state at External, and T.W. MacDermott, the under secretary, who had recommended Massey to Prime Minister Louis St. Laurent. (McDermott was the father of Galt McDermott, the composer of *Hair*, which had its first performance eighteen years later). Archie was known in Ottawa for his first-class mind, his urbane wit, his organizational skills, his charm—he liked women and women liked him—and his generous drinking habit.

"What do you mean—'trouble shooting'," I asked.

"I mean what I say," Archie replied professorially. "We are having a little trouble and we want you to shoot it down. We know you're a good shot."

"If I say yes," I warned him, "it doesn't mean that I'm prepared to do anything illegal."

"No, murder wouldn't be part of your job specs," he replied solemnly.

"Good. Then, what *are* the requirements?"

"A good nose, that's all. You may have heard that a few people recently received anonymous letters in the mail, saying some unsavoury things about us. We want you to find out who is writing them."

I had not heard of the letters.

"Unsavoury things?" I asked. "Are they true?"

"The problem is—yes. Which makes us think that the writer is ... let us say ... unusually well connected."

"Maybe one of the commissioners?"

"That is highly unlikely," he laughed. "May I make a suggestion? Come over for a drink at my place on Second Avenue and I will show you one of the letters. There are several more, but I keep them at the office. Then you can decide whether you would like to take this on."

I told him I would come the following Tuesday. The commission under discussion was ponderously called the Royal Commission on National Development of the Arts, Letters and Sciences, but it was universally known as the Massey Commission. The government wished, "to have a survey made of institutions, agencies and organizations which expressed national feeling, promoted common under-standing and added to the variety and richness of Canadian life," and to examine cultural institutions, broadcasting and relations with voluntary associations and to consider federal university scholarships.

Vincent Massey, now sixty-two, was the grandson of the founder of the company that later became Massey-

Harris, the world-renowned manufacturer of agricultural equipment. He had been at loose ends since he returned in 1946 from his posting as high commissioner in London, where he had been since 1935. Before that he had been minister (i.e., ambassador) in Washington. Not only as a high-level public servant and life-long Liberal, but also as a patron of the arts—among others of the Hart House String Quartet—he was the obvious choice. Massey was a personal friend of many artists and musicians throughout the country, and an art collector on a lavish scale. He was also the author of *On Being Canadian*.

On Tuesday I went over to Archie's place. After he had mixed the martinis, he picked up a typewritten letter and handed it to me. Then he went to the kitchen where I heard him putting away the dishes, leaving me alone with the letter.

Mr. A.L. O'Connor
Art Gallery of Prince Edward Island
Charlottetown, Prince Edward Island
Dear Mr. O'Connor,
I am writing to a small number of prominent Canadians who care deeply about this country, as I do. My purpose is to make sure that the next time the government launches a royal commission on cultural matters it will appoint the right commissioners and choose a more humble chairman. Even his old friend Mackenzie King accused Vincent Massey of self-aggrandizement. In earlier years they had been on excellent terms. Massey was one of the few who was allowed to call him by his nickname "Rex." (My sources are absolutely foolproof.) Massey is a man whose ideals are those of the British aristocracy and not those of modern, forward-looking

Canada. Even Viscount Cranbourne, the Seventh Marquess of Salisbury, observed, "Vincent is a fine chap but he makes one feel a bit of a savage." That is exactly the point: appointing him was like asking Louis XVI to be the head of a regiment of twentieth-century boy scouts.

I happen to know that when St. Laurent first sounded Massey out about becoming chairman of the commission he confided to him that he was being considered as the first Canadian-born governor general when Lord Alexander's time was up. As a matter of fact, there was nobody else on his list. (You may remember that the intention to have this commission had already been mentioned in the Speech from the Throne.) St. Laurent told him that taking on the chairmanship was a good preparation for him while at the same time introducing him to the country. So from then on, naturally, Massey felt like the heir apparent. Because that is what he was.

I am not the first person to observe that Vincent Massey is a better actor than his brother Raymond. Acting is the art of dissembling. He is very skilled at pretending not to preach culture to the natives. He never uses the word. I myself have heard Massey say, privately, "Unfortunately there is no synonym in the English language for culture. It is a normal term in French. Its meaning is perfectly understood but translated into English it produces an uncomfortable self-consciousness."

To make us comfortable he has to dissemble.

I wish he had accepted the mastership of his old Oxford college, Balliol, when Lord Samuel offered it to him a couple of yeas ago. That would have been a straightforward thing for him to do, very suitable for him. He would not have to dissemble and play the role of the common man.

You will hear from me again.

Signed: Anonymous

Not a bad letter, I thought.

"Another martini?" Archie asked, when he finally reappeared.

"That would be very nice, thank you."

I handed him my glass, wondering whether I should keep him dangling for a bit or tell him right away that I would be happy to accept his offer.

"I don't approve of writing anonymous letters," I said, just in order to say something. "Though under certain circumstances it's perhaps not a bad idea. Especially if one wants to hurt somebody without being hurt oneself. But one has to have strong reasons. I mean, it's a lot of work, deciding what to say, how to put it, who to send it to, finding out people's addresses. And—buying the stamps. Who has the time? For all we know, Mr. O'Connor is one of dozens recipients of the same letter."

"That's what we want you to find out. Will you do it? We'd give you a research contract for a month. As to the real purpose of your assignment, we would rely on your discretion."

"Of course," I said, "we know a little about the writer already. He is, as you say, unusually well connected."

"He or she," Archie corrected me.

"Yes. Good point. But 'he' is more likely, you must admit. How many women would know that Massey used to call Mackenzie King Rex, and then boast about their foolproof sources? And know what St. Laurent said to him in a private conversation? Not his cleaning lady, surely."

"Careful! You must not make any assumptions. Anyway, as Horace used to say, *dimidium facti qui coepit habet*."

"And what does that mean?"

"He who has begun has the work half done."

"I promise nothing, but I should have the answer in a couple of weeks."

"Come and see me tomorrow in my office, say, at three. I'll give the remaining letters to you and introduce you to a few people."

❦　　❦　　❦

This is the second letter.

Dr. Arthur McGreevy
College of Architectural Design
Vancouver, British Columbia
　　Dear Dr. McGreevy,
　　I have been told that you are as unhappy as many other Canadians about the way the Massey Commission is going. If my information is correct, you have singled out Norman MacKenzie as the Achilles heel of the commission. You are absolutely right. It is a great puzzle why he was chosen since, as you know, he has never shown the slightest interest in cultural or artistic matters. He has this in common with Mackenzie King, who also has no taste for the arts and sciences. That is why we never had a Massey Commission when he was prime minister. If he had seen a political advantage in one, he would no doubt have done so. St. Laurent, on the other hand, has a genuine interest in these matters and is not merely concerned about accommodating the cultural and scientific elites.
　　Norman MacKenzie is an eminent international lawyer and has an unusually distinguished war record, having spent four years in the trenches, escaping death by miracles and earning the Military Cross and Bar. Above all, he was a successful president of the University of New Brunswick, and is

now much respected as a capable and hard-working president of the University of British Columbia. The only part of the commission's mandate, however, about which he is qualified to speak as an expert is the matter of federal financing of universities. He feels deeply that we need it and has given it a great deal of thought, especially to the contentious matter of federal scholarships. On this topic he has clashed repeatedly with the super-elitist Hilda Neatby, taking the populist line in arguing that gifted young people without adequate means must be given the chance to attend university. This, he thinks, must be given the highest priority. Neatby prefers to put the emphasis on excellence, not access.

No doubt MacKenzie was chosen for the simple reason that he has many friends in the higher echelons of Ottawa. The fact that he represents both coasts—as you know, he was born in Pugwash, Nova Scotia—was no doubt an additional reason for his appointment.

I am confident that you will join many other concerned Canadians in making sure that the government will ignore whatever recommendations will emerge from this ill-conceived commission.

Yours sincerely,
Signed: Anonymous

  ❧ ❧ ❧

I made a point of not spending too much time in the Laurentian Building in Ottawa, which housed the commission. I did not want to draw attention to my detective work. But I did pick up some gossip that I thought might turn out to be useful. I discovered, for example, that a number of wartime refugees from Nazi-occupied Europe held a grudge against Vincent Massey because they thought he had not been sufficiently sympathetic to their plight and held up their immigration to Canada, which came through only after he had left to return home. But it was unlikely, although not impossible, that they had already acquired the inside knowledge that Anonymous obviously possessed. I also discovered that two or three top people in the scientific community had made it known that they believed they could make important contributions to the commission and implied that they hoped, perhaps even expected, to be appointed. They felt slighted when they received polite acknowledgements but nothing more. If none of them was Anonymous perhaps one their wives was.

Dr. McGreevy's reference to Mackenzie King's reluctance to launch a Massey Commission gave me another idea that first struck me as absurdly far-fetched but, on second thought, was perhaps worth pondering. Could it be that Mackenzie King was Anonymous? If not he, perhaps it was one of his secretaries or one of his friends in the spiritual underworld? Clearly he had no use for Vincent Massey, even though many decades ago they had been good friends. He had indeed accused Massey of "self-aggrandizement" and it was known that when Massey was high commissioner in London there was frequently tension between the two. King disliked Massey's Anglophilia, both on political and personal grounds. But there was another possible motive. Surely King hated his successor, the way Queen Victoria hated her successor, who became Edward VII. That hatred seems to be endemic in the relationship between anybody in power and his or her successor. And now St. Laurent was going to get credit for something King had refused to do. So naturally King would do anything he could to undermine it.

Mrs. Mary Whitehead
Department of Adult Education
University of Moose Jaw, Saskatchewan
  Dear Mrs. Whitehead,
  May I say how much I appreciated your recent criticism of Professor Hilda Neatby. You say you were a former student of Miss Neatby's and that she had been a major influence in your life. Now you are disappointed in her because you find her pose as a simple farm girl deplorable. You quote her as saying to the editor of the women's page in the local Victoria paper that she is really a Saskatchewan farm woman at heart. "I can milk a cow," you quote her as saying, "take care of the chickens, and I think I could even help with the ploughing."
  I agree: these remarks are disingenuous and designed to mislead.
  Why, you ask, can't elitists admit to being elitists? The same excellent question could be asked about Vincent Massey, who deliberately avoids the word "culture" in his public remarks. I have not heard him go as far as to say that he was a man of the people. These "just folks" poses touch on the nature of the society in which we live. It tends to equate democracy with egalitarianism.
  Hilda Neatby has much to be proud of and you are to be envied for having been a student of hers. Did she ever mention in class that she and her eight siblings were brought up on a farm in Earl Grey, in your province of Saskatchewan, in great poverty? And that she was two when her family came over from England—her father having been a doctor who gave up medicine for farming once they were here? And that he read to his children regularly and that both her parents were determined to make sure that their children received the best possible education? Probably not. Probably she did not

*wish to waste time on irrelevant personal matters. Striving
towards excellence—and emulating the super-elitist Matthew
Arnold—came first.*

I enjoyed your comments.

With best wishes,

Signed: Anonymous

Matthew Arnold! The austere Victorian poet and critic and
son of Thomas Arnold, the famous headmaster of Rugby!
His definition of culture was the guideline for Neatby
and for Massey: culture is to know the best that has been
said and thought in the world. In their view it was up
to the authorities—up to the state—to lead the masses
towards knowledge and wisdom. That is what they both
believed and that this was why Vincent Massey relied on
Hilda Neatby for many of his key decisions. No wonder
that she neither liked nor respected the populist Norman
MacKenzie.

Of the five commissioners, Neatby was the only one to
take a leave of absence from her regular job. She conscien-
tiously attended all the sessions. Hardly a typical course
of action for a farm girl.

How fortunate that she spoke excellent French, having
studied at the Sorbonne and later specialized in Quebec
history. Naturally she had excellent relations with her
colleague the Dominican Father Georges-Henri Lévesque,
who addressed her in their correspondence as *ma chère
soeur* and refers to her as *my Presbyterian boss* while she
calls him *my catholic padre.* (They were the only unmar-
ried commissioners.)

I learned much later, in fact, that Neatby played a lead-
ing role in writing the commission's report. It became the

precursor of a book she published a year or two later, which was an attack on progressive education that she called *So Little for the Mind.*

That was all very well, but is Matthew Arnold a clue? Yes, as a matter of fact, I decided he was, however bizarre this seemed. Matthew Arnold was the grandfather of the novelist Aldous Huxley, who was later the author of *Brave New World.* Huxley was known to use mescaline to stimulate his imagination. I concluded that Anonymous was a drug dealer who would follow up his letters to sell this soft drug. I would freely admit that this clue had only a remote chance of being useful, but at this stage nothing could be ruled out.

Professor Sylvstre Duval
Collège Jean Baptiste
Sorel, Quebec
  Dear Professor Duval,
    [This letter is a translation from French.]
    I see from the letter you wrote to the editor of Le Devoir *that as someone who firmly supports the purposes of the Massey Commission you consider the appointment of Father Lévesque a grave political error. May I echo this view and offer my support in making your position known throughout the country, and especially in your province, even though circumstances do not allow me to disclose my identity. I can say, however, that I share with Father Lévesque his devotion to the humanist tradition and to Christian values, and I share the conviction that our society must be guided by a morality grounded in faith. I am also convinced, as is Father Lévesque, that this conviction provides the common ground for both French and English cultures in Canada.*

Why then do I agree with you so wholeheartedly? Perhaps you will allow me to spell out my agreement in terms that go a little further than you do in your Letter to the Editor.

As dean of the faculty of social science at Laval University, Father Lévesque is known as an open antagonist of Premier Maurice Duplessis, who is solidly opposed to the "radical" reforms to which Father Lévesque has devoted his academic career. Father Lévesque's role will make it impossible for Duplessis to implement any of the commission's recommendations. Why deprive Quebeckers of the benefits that the commission will recommend from an arts council to support artists, musicians and writers, to a similar council to aid scientific research, to federal grants to universities including scholarships, to all kinds of other support for the humanities and sciences, such as archives and libraries? Duplessis will say no to all of this, in the name of provincial autonomy in culture and education. Was this provocation really necessary? Was it necessary to appoint someone who openly supports the asbestos strike and who trains union organizers in his faculty, someone who is the animating spirit of the cooperative movement that is anathema to the premier? Could they not have given the job to a retired judge, or a former ambassador, or an under-employed senator from Quebec?

I know, of course, why Father Lévesque was appointed. He is a personal friend of Prime Minister St. Laurent. Both taught at Laval University at the same time. I understand that Father Lévesque had to be persuaded, that he said he did not think his English was good enough and that he simply did not have the time. He accepted finally only on condition that it was understood he was a Quebecker before he was a Canadian but that he was thoroughly opposed to Duplessis's narrow-minded nationalism. St. Laurent replied that the commission was a positive way to counter it and a way to open up the province to a wider culture. You may not know, but I have heard it from entirely reliable sources, that much later Father Lévesque was particularly impressed by a special study written for the commission by Vincent Massey's nephew, the philosopher George Grant. He argued that a belief in God was fundamental to the rational pursuit of the good life. Grant made it clear that by "good life" he did not mean indulgence in luxuries but an existence that was wholly informed by humanism based on faith.

Humanism, even if it was Christian, was not a word that would endear the commission to Premier Duplessis and his friends in the church.

As you suggested, ways should been found to meet the objectives of the commission without, from the very outset, depriving Quebeckers of its benefactions.

I know you and I are on the same wavelength, if I may borrow a word from broadcasting, another vital concern of the commission since it affects all Canadians, the educated and the uneducated, the Christians and the non-Christians.

I will do all I can, in my modest way, to make your views known across the country.

Signed: Anonymous

I had given myself two weeks to find out who Anonymous was. On the evening before my self-imposed term was up, I was the guest at a memorable dinner party in the apartment of my employer, Archie Day, the secretary of the commission. Of course, not a word was said about my secret assignment, but I am sure he was as aware of my deadline as I was.

The very alcoholic dinner was memorable for three

reasons. One, it was hosted by Archie's current girlfriend, the delightful Melanie Smith who was a filmmaker at the National Film Board and who told many amusing stories about her boss, the legendary John Grierson, the Scottish celebrity who coined the term "documentary." In 1939 Mackenzie King had invited them to launch the NFB to make Canada's role in the war effort known at home and abroad. Grierson had recruited a number of gifted bohemians (few of whom had ever made a film before) of a kind Ottawa had never seen before. Among them were a number of Archie's former girlfriends.

The second reason why this dinner was so memorable was that George Grant was there, Vincent Massey's nephew to whom the last letter had referred. He was the life of the party, rotund and blue-eyed, a most entertaining, witty, charming philosopher whose main characteristic (apart from his sloppy appearance) was his boyish enthusiasm for the many causes and ideas that attracted him. He raved about Mozart, especially about *Don Giovanni*, the great lover who ended up in Hell, although there was not a man alive, he said, who did not identify himself with him. There was a Don Giovanni in everyone of us, especially in our host, Archie Day. The National Film Board, George Grant added, was full of ladies whom Archie had loved and abandoned, ladies who still loved him and would flock back to him at a wink.

"I'll strangle each one of them," Melanie observed with feeling.

"Now, now, now," Archie said, pouring her another glass of wine. "There's no need to go that far. You know that I don't like violence. Just a little word of discouragement will do the trick, I'm sure."

"I am by no means sure at all," George Grant said, laughing while trying to remove a stain from the front of his jacket, which badly needed cleaning. "There is a gorgeous film editor I met the other day. She came from Spain, like Don Giovanni, and her name was Carmelita Diaz. She told me, referring to you. Archie, in her ravishing English, with fire in her black eyes, 'In my country we have many ways to do a revenge.' She was Donna Anna, miraculously reincarnated. *Ah, vendicar, se il puoi, giura quel sangue ognor!* [Ah, swear to avenge that blood if you can!]" George Grant sang the entire aria, slightly out of tune, while Archie, expressionless, stared into space.

That was the third reason, just in the nick of time.

To Mr. Colin McKay,
Manager, Station CGHY
Lucky Lake, British Columbia
  Dear Mr. McKay,
  May I present to you my strongest commendation for speaking out publicly against the way the Massy Commission has been set up. No wonder that in its discussion of broadcasting it is so brazenly pro-CBC and so shamelessly loaded against the interests of private broadcasters like yourself. How could it be otherwise when a man like Vincent Massey had the last word on the appointments? Every one, with only one exception—not counting Vincent Massey—is an academic. No wonder the one exception, the civil engineer and businessman Arthur Surveyer is having such a difficult time. He does not speak the same language as the others. But, strangely enough, as far as I can see, he does not disagree with the commission's overall view that the most important mission of broadcasting, public and private, is to elevate the masses.

The reason Arthur Surveyer was chosen was that he is a prominent Montrealer with an excellent record of public service, with many close connections to the English-speaking business community, and heavily involved in hydro-electric developments in Quebec. He is therefore thoroughly at home in the world of modern technology. In that world the other commissioners are, of course, aliens. With television around the corner, no doubt the government thought his expertise would be invaluable. This remains to be seen.

In the internal discussions among the commissioners Arthur Surveyer is unlikely to be strong enough to convince his colleagues that they must listen to men like yourself. For one thing, he is seventy-two years old and not in the best of health. The test is the question of regulation. You argue—in my opinion rightly—that it is intolerable for the CBC, which also sells time to advertisers, to regulate its competitors. You insist that the CBC must not be an umpire and a player at the same time. But will the commission take the regulatory function away from the CBC? You and I doubt it. They will accept the prevailing view, that the primary function of private broadcasters like yourself is to distribute the signal of the national public broadcaster to the country at large. Therefore you have to be subsidiary. I agree that this is profoundly undemocratic especially at a time when western democracies are being challenged every day by the men in the Kremlin. The cause of democracy is not served by a system that thrives at the expense of the common man, not for his benefit.

You say you would also like to devote your life to elevating the masses if you could afford it. Whenever you carry the CBC's cultural programs, you say, you lose touch with your audience. Your listeners prefer Bob Hope and ball games. My heart bleeds for you.

Please continue to speak out. Please continue to challenge the commission's colossal cultural snobbery.
I will do all I can to support you.
Signed: Anonymous

I needed proof that Carmelita Diaz was Anonymous. So, on the morning after the dinner party, I went to the former ramshackle factory, not far from Rideau Hall, that was now the National Film Board. I told the man at the desk I was a researcher for the Massey Commission and asked whether I could see her for a minute.

Very soon she sat opposite me in a little office near the entrance. Carmelita was just as George Grant had described her—gorgeous and dark-eyed. Obviously I could not ask her directly if she wrote these letters. So I said the commission was dealing with the mandate of the National Film Board, and I had been told she was editing the series *Canada Carries On*. I was wondering whether perhaps I could see some of the footage.

She looked right through me.

"Did Archie send you?" she said, her eyes blazing.

"No," I replied, firmly. "He does not know I am here. Nor why."

"But I know!" she shouted. "You are here because of the letters."

George Grant had not told me how intelligent she was. I confessed.

"I hope Archie has suffered," she said, exuding pure hatred. "All he ever talked about was that stupid commission. I hope I hit him where it hurts."

"You did," I assured her. "But tell me, how did you get all that information? How did you know what to write?"

"Simple. I have many friends who know these things. I told them I was writing articles for a Spanish paper. They also helped me with my English. They said I was not committing a crime since everything I wrote was true."

"Absolutely," I agreed.

I was going to add that I was sure Archie will quickly recover from his suffering. But that was probably the last thing she wanted to hear.

Archie was dumbfounded when I made my report.

All he could do was to exclaim:

"As Ovid used to say, *dulce puella mala est* [so sweet a plague is woman]!"

The Fall of Andrew Allan

In 1953, I at last met Andrew Allan. I had heard of him for more than ten years, as the mastermind behind the CBC's radio plays to which I listened every Sunday night and discussed with friends every Monday morning, like everybody else I knew. Since 1944 he had created—on radio—the first coast-to-coast theatre in Canada. And—who knows?—last year's opening of the Stratford Shakespearian Festival may turn out to be an event of comparable importance, although it cannot by its very nature benefit every Canadian, even in the most remote regions, as Andrew's plays do.

He was forty-five and could easily have been the father of many of the brash young producers and script and production assistants who had been hired in the last year or two for the CBC's brand-new television service. They wore turtleneck sweaters, wore jeans or slacks, and spoke a lingo of their own designed to be unintelligible by normal people.

Andrew was tall and handsome, had an unusually high forehead, with a pale pink boyish face and strikingly blue eyes. He was by nature formal. I was told he could be irascible and moody. A tireless perfectionist, he never raised his voice, never argued and was invariably polite. But when he was displeased with somebody's performance, inside and outside the studio, he just stared at the offender—a terrifying experience. Arthur Hill spoke for quite a few fellow actors when he said, "I love working for Andrew, but I hate him." Barbara Kelly said he had ruined performing for her. "He would not accept one single error. I found him an unbelievably hard and nasty taskmaster."

During rehearsals he addressed his actors formally by their surnames—Mr., Mrs. or Miss X—even though some of them, such as John Drainie, Bernard Braden and Lister Sinclair, were close personal friends who had followed him from Vancouver to Toronto in 1944. His authority was absolute.

In his productions all the subtleties of a stage performance were narrowed down to the instrument of the voice. Inflections, intonations, class and regional accents combined with sound effects and music freed the listeners' imagination from the limitations of visual reality. This served only one purpose: to convey the writer's intentions. For Andrew the script was sacrosanct and he took endless pains to encourage his writers and find new ones. He also made sure that they, and his actors, were adequately paid.

All this began when Andrew and his crew arrived in Toronto from the West Coast to launch *Stage 44*. He had once prophesized that "broadcasting was Canada's principal means of survival."

He was born in Scotland in 1907, the son of a restless clergyman who took his family to Australia, New York, Peterborough and Toronto. He went to the University of Toronto during the Depression. There he wrote for the *Varsity* and acted on stage with drama groups, but never finished his degree. Money was tight and he felt he should pay his own way. So he took odd jobs and eventually became a junior radio announce at CFRB, a position that required hosting duties as well as writing continuity, soap operas and radio plays. The job was exhilarating but exhausting. In the winter of 1938 he booked a passage to England on the spur of the moment. For two years he further refined his technical skills and worked for Radio Luxembourg and Radio Normandie. In 1939 his father visited him. Immediately after the outbreak of the war, invited by the CBC to produce radio drama in Vancouver, he was aboard the *Athenia* bound for Canada when she was torpedoed. The date was September third. Andrew, his father and the American actress Judith Evelyn initially made it to safety, but their lifeboat was thrashed by the propeller of a freighter that had come to pick up survivors. Andrew and Evelyn clung to a fragment of the lifeboat in the cold and dark Irish sea. His father drowned.

Andrew was unable to speak about the experience until thirty years later.

꜡   ꜡   ꜡

Now at last I met him face to face. It was a crucial time in his life, when the exciting new medium of television was attracting everybody's attention. How could *he* resist? Many of his colleagues had already made the transition.

At the time, I was an assistant to Fergus Mutrie, the CBC's director of television in Toronto. I got the job because he and my father were members of the Arts and Letters Club. My father always thought it a good idea to start work at the top of an organization rather than at the bottom.

My duties were to represent Ferg, as he was universally known, at meetings for which he did not have the time or to which he did not wish to go, and to deal tactfully with complaining members of the public and with hopeful job applicants.

I met Andrew first at a meeting called by the Technical Department on the second floor of the television building on Jarvis Street, next to the television tower, across the parking lot from the old radio building. The purpose of the meeting was to discuss the requirements for Andrew's forthcoming debut as a television producer the following Tuesday. (There was no distinction between producer and director in CBC television—all producers had to have the skill and self-confidence to direct live shows in the studio. Videotaping had not yet been invented.) He had brought his indispensable assistant, Alice Frick, with him. She was his script reader and conducted all the negotiations for performing rights for him. My function was to offer Ferg's help if any difficulties had to be resolved. The meeting was attended by lighting and sound people, as well as representatives from the design and staging areas.

Andrew was not used to attending other people's meetings. In radio he had total control over every aspect of his productions, artistic and technical, over scripts, casting, performance and music. In this new situation he had made up his mind to do all he could to live by the rules of the new medium. His conduct was impeccable. Everything went smoothly and Ferg's intervention was not required.

There was, of course, a marked difference in style between Andrew and the others. He wore an elegant grey suit with a white handkerchief in the breast pocket and a maroon tie. The technical people were in shirt sleeves.

After the meeting I walked back to the radio building with him and Alice. We were stopped en route by Mavor

Moore, the chief producer, himself an eminent writer and actor, and also a good personal friend of Andrew's. I knew he had encouraged him to make the jump.

"How did it go?" Mavor asked. "I'm sorry I couldn't be there."

"It went without a hitch," Andrew replied, speaking as usual with precision. "I think we are in pretty good shape. All the pieces are in place. Come and join us for a cup of coffee."

We went to the cafeteria in the basement.

I had met Mavor several times in Ferg's office, and had also seen his bald head and expressive features in one or two of the plays CBC Television had presented in its first season (1952–53), perhaps in Morley Callaghan's *To Tell the Truth*, Ted Allan's *The Money Makers* or Robertson Davies' *Fortune, My Foe*. In 1952 there was no network as yet; there was, on the English side, only CBLT Toronto on Channel 9. Transmissions began at five p.m. and the last show was scheduled at nine-thirty.

"So you've been assigned to smooth the way across the River Styx?" Mavor said to me.

Fortunately I happened to remember that the River Styx in Greek mythology is the river separating earth from the underworld, i.e., Hades.

"Oh," I laughed, "it turned out to be quite a friendly little stream."

"Good." Mavor said. He turned to Andrew. "How are the rehearsals going?"

"I've finished the blocking," he said. "Everything has been written down. Penny has been a great help."

Penny Goodman was the script assistant who had drama experience.

"And," Andrew continued, "I learned a lot from watching other directors at work."

"I am glad. The best training, of course, is doing hockey. But maybe it's just as well that you were spared that. If we make mistakes, so what? It's not the end of the world. By the way, you were right to have chosen Len's play. Not too many actors, a simple set and only a few scene changes."

Andrew had chosen Len Peterson's *They're All Afraid*, which he had produced on radio in his first season, the last year of the war, on *Stage 44*. It is a play about office bullying and fear, and had been criticized for not raising morale in wartime. For that reason it had also displeased the CBC's executive vice-president Ernie Bushnell. But last spring it received a top award at an American drama festival and Bushnell had to eat crow when he accepted it.

"You know, Mavor," Andrew said, "I had a terrible time making up my mind. On close inspection, few of the plays I have done lend themselves to television. They were written for the ear, not for the eye. I nearly chose an abridged version of *The Importance of Being Ernest*. It is always a surefire hit. But it would have been hopelessly wrong and misleading."

"It certainly would," Mavor agreed. "Unless you pretended that Oscar Wilde was a new writer from Winnipeg you had discovered."

On Tuesday, the day of the show, Andrew was the very model of self-control. If he was nervous he did not show it. He allowed Alice and me to stand behind him in the control room. For the first few minutes everything went well, but then I noticed—and so did Alice—that when he said "Camera One" he meant Camera Two, and so on. Penny discovered immediately that she had to ignore his commands. She had a marked-up script and eyes in her head and took over. It was impossible to believe that Andrew himself did not notice he had lost control. But he was such a respected figure and the situation was so sensitive that everybody pretended he had remained in charge.

At the end of the show he did something unprecedented. Without saying a word he took Penny's hand and kissed it. In return she kissed him on the cheek.

      ❧   ❧   ❧

Andrew carried on with his *Stage* series on radio and remained supervisor of drama until 1955. But the excitement had evaporated as audiences shifted to television. His team gradually disintegrated and the writers and actors found new opportunities.

Andrew deplored television's constricting lack of reliance on words—that is, on writers. He understood that television production was team work and that, even if he had succeeded, he would never have been able to exercise the absolute authority he had in the old medium. So for a time he had to be satisfied with radio. He later recalled, "I had spent a dozen years learning the skills I need for radio drama and I didn't feel I had that kind of time for television." In 1957 he was fifty.

Bad years followed. He began drinking. His second marriage dissolved. It took several years until his old friends in radio came to his rescue and commissioned short pieces and essays.

In 1974 Andrew Allan died.

"No age is called golden until it is long past," he wrote. "To survive you need a good capacity to absorb disappointments."